"YOU WON'T FIND MY NAME ON THE GLASS DOOR BECAUSE THERE IS NO GLASS DOOR, AND THE ONLY KIND OF KILLING I LIKE TO GET INVOLVED IN IS WHEN THE BODY'S ALREADY BEEN GLUED BACK TOGETHER AND THE ORGANIST AT FOREST LAWN IS PLAYING 'NEARER, MY GOD, TO THEE.'

"ON MY CARD IT SAYS: *PUBLIC RELATIONS*. THAT'LL GIVE YOU AN IDEA HOW TIMES HAVE CHANGED."

He's B. F. Cage—
laid back private eye of the Seventies

"Breezy . . . expertly written. . . . Nobody will be bored."
The New York Times

"First-rate, bullet-fast . . . as strong, tough and violent a suspense novel as any reader is likely to want."
Nashville Tennesseean

"Corruption slithering out of every pool-side villa in California. There isn't a wasted word here. Good reading."
West Coast Review of Books

HUSH MONEY

PETER ISRAEL

AVON
PUBLISHERS OF BARD, CAMELOT AND DISCUS BOOKS

AVON BOOKS
A division of
The Hearst Corporation
959 Eighth Avenue
New York, New York 10019

Published by arrangement with Thomas Y. Crowell Co., Inc.
Library of Congress Catalog Card Number: 74-8992
ISBN: 0-380-01793-8

First Avon Printing, November, 1977

Printed in the U.S.A.

For all my friends, and one especially

Prologue

Maybe somewhere in Los Angeles you can still find the kind of private eye you used to read about in novels. You know the type: hat back on his head, feet up on the desk, a bottle of whiskey in the drawer and a day-old beard on his phiz. Hangs out downtown in one of those seedy old buildings, the ones with the elevator cages out in the courtyards, and on one side of him there's a chiropractor fronting for a lonely hearts racket and on the other a one-eyed dealer in rare coins. He talks tough, acts tougher, but deep down inside he's got a heart as soft as an oyster. Blondes go for him, also little old ladies with millions in their mattresses, also his secretary (played by Ann Blyth).

Maybe you could at that. Trouble is, they've torn down half of the downtown for a Kinney parking and what's left has been so chichi'd up that Philip Marlowe couldn't afford the down payment on a broom closet. The chiropractor's moved back to Fresno, the last time I saw Ann Blyth she was hustling a savings and loan association on TV, and those widows who used to walk in just when the lonesome stallion was dictating his memoirs now take their business elsewhere.

To shysters, for instance.

Or CPAs, or investment counselors, or head-shrinkers.

Or even me, now and then, but you won't find my name on the glass door because there is no glass door, and the only kind of killing I like to get involved in is when the body's already been glued back together and the organist at Forest Lawn is playing "Nearer, My God, to Thee." Sure I've got the heart of gold, too, but there's only one person in this cruel world who knows the combination, and his name happens to be Cage.

So's mine.

On my card it says: Public Relations. That'll give you an idea how times have changed.

Which isn't to say California's all that different from the one Mr. Marlowe hung around in. Right, we've had a movie star for governor and you can get a fix in the local high school if that's your pleasure, or laid or blown or flagellated in any old neighborhood massage parlor. There's television instead of radio, Toyotas instead of Lincoln Zephyrs, and everybody wears long hair, including the quarterbacks of the L.A. Rams. But the crimes are still the same—murder, rape, extortion, you name it—and so's the system: a few people squeezing the many for money, without the many catching on to how it works.

Look at it this way. There are only two kinds of California people: those who've got it and those who want it. Those who've got it also want something else, call it peace or respectability, and the rest are willing to give them all the something else they can buy. On the one hand, the oil rich, the land rich, the inherited rich, the just plain filthy California rich; on the other, that army of scavengers and bloodsuckers: cops, shysters, politicians, judges, insurance investigators, newspapermen and just plain garden-variety blackmailers. More business goes on between the two kinds than you'd imagine, some of it even legal, but you'll never find the one hobnobbing in the laundromat with the other.

Which is where I come in.

Hush money, you could call it. The cover-up, the fix. Greasing the Wheels of Progress.

The gathering and suppression of information, better known as Public Relations.

It's not the cleanest work in the world, I'll admit, or the most moral, but the morality went out of me the night I shit in my pants up at the Ch'ongch'on, the winter of '50, and I'll take what's left over. I've got money in the bank, four wheels with air conditioning, a closetful of clothes, a pantryful of booze, and I know where enough of the bodies are buried to keep it all going till the earthquake dumps us into the Pacific. I get to sleep nights. In the mornings I can look down on the sweaty masses getting ready for another day in the meat-grinder, and all I have to do to change the view is cross the living room and watch the waves rolling in against the Santa Monica cliffs, much like they must have when Colonel Frémont was still in knickers.

So if it's Marlowe or Archer you're looking for, good luck to you, but I'd say your best bet these days would be to head for the corner drugstore and pick yourself up a paperback for a buck.

And friend, that's the last piece of free advice you'll get from yours truly.

1

The call had come in while I was down at the tennis courts. The biddy from the answering service gave me the rundown. There were the usual cats and dogs: some number called Karen who'd been trying to get through to me for two weeks, a custom car guy who wanted to show me something he'd worked out with the Mazda rotary, plus an urgent-urgent from a Mr. Curie of Curie, Etc., Etc. & Curie, attorneys-at-law in Beverly Hills.

The biddy was pushing this Karen. She said she'd gotten to know her over the phone. She had a lovely voice, she said. I didn't remember any Karen I wanted to remember and the Mazda rotary could wait for a rainy Saturday, but after showering down and a sandwich-and-Heineken's on the terrace, I got on the blower with George S. Curie III's English-speaking secretary. Verry.

"No, I'm teddibly sorry Mr. Cage, it's not something Mr. Curie will discuss over the telephone. But could you come round this afternoon, say at five sharp?"

"Time for tea?" I said.

"Could you come at five then?"

You could feel the frost on the hedgerows.

Yes I could, I said, and did.

It was in one of those little side streets off Doheny, a Tudoresque manse built for a family of twenty or so but discreet enough by California standards, with a putting-green lawn and a well-tended garden sloping up behind it and a discreet gold plaque by the front door with discreet engraving on it. Most of the high-powered legal talent these days hang out in the high rises along Wilshire or the Avenue of the Stars (sic) in Century City, but a few of the really class ones have gone English with a vengeance. A question of clientele. The Curies pander to the L.A. nobility, hell they belong to it, and the L.A. nobility still has a lot of trouble with its ancestry. To hear them tell it, the *Mayflower* must've been the size of the *Queen Mary*, but for the overflow, who do they have to trace themselves back to, the Donner Party? So they deck themselves out with "solicitors" in Savile Row clothes and discreet castles, and if the shysters in question have never been nearer to Oxford or Cambridge than the campus of U.S.C., well, their secretaries will have to do.

There have always been two Curies, one at the top of the masthead, one at the bottom. For all I know they do it that way to save on stationery. The one time I worked for them before, my Curie, the III, was at the bottom. I never met the II, but I heard him clumping around in the attic overhead. Now he'd gone on to that big law firm in the sky, the III had taken over the top spot and presumably there was a IV around somewhere, even if they only had him licking stamps in the mailroom.

Nothing else had changed except the receptionist, who was too good to have come from anywhere east of Riverside. We admired each other quietly for about thirty seconds until the secretary lunged through a door, swinging her glasses like a field hockey stick. She doubletimed me down some steps and up some others into the library, a paneled affair with portraits on the walls and law volumes in glassed-in cases which looked like fake fronts but weren't, black leather armchairs and a discreet portable bar in one corner. A minute later to the second George S. Curie III slipped in, and he shook my hand as though he'd just touched a dishrag in a pile of clean handkerchiefs.

No, nothing had changed.

He sat across from me in that tired civilized way of the English club member who crossed his legs the day Chamberlain signed at Munich and hasn't uncrossed them since. The gray suit he wore, with vest, mightn't have been Savile Row at that but it wasn't Hongkong either. His hair was a little grayer, his cheeks had that pale gray sheen which made you think the barber had just gone out the back door, but the accent was one Charles Dickens never heard.

Pure California, you'd have to say.

"Do you read the newspapers?" he said.

I nodded.

"I watch TV too," I answered.

"Then you already know about the Beydon business? Karen Beydon? The girl they call Karie?"

I guess it was my day for Karens, but you'd have had to be deaf and blind and constipated for the last forty-eight hours not to have heard of this one.

He sighed for the record and put on the expression of a mortician who's just laid out his mother.

We stared at each other.

"A terrible tragedy," he said, lowering his eyes. "An only child, and the mother died less than three years ago, did you know that? She was lovely too, Karen I mean—Karie—the pictures don't begin to do her justice. And gifted. I understand she wrote poetry, did you know that? Poor Twink—I'm talking about Philip Beydon—I've never seen him buckle under pressure, but he doesn't know which way to turn right now. It's understandable, God knows. A man loses his wife, then his daughter, and for it to happen this terrible way, well . . ."

I guess if he'd worn glasses he'd have been wiping them about then. As is, he pursed his lips at me, and then the rest of the sigh went out of him.

He had little to add to the newspaper accounts, at least in the version he gave me, and he left out some of the less savory details and speculations, including my own. Maybe it's no longer news these days when a kid jumps—or falls or is pushed—out a window, but when the kid is a Beydon and a Diehl and the family that spawned her has been in and out of the local blatts for years, not just the obits and the society columns but the financial section, even sports (I'd read something somewhere about "Twink" Beydon organizing a California challenge to the America Cup), then it's news all right, at least by L.A. standards. The more so since the window happened to be on the seventh floor of a brand new mixed dormitory, property of the Regents of the University of California. The more so since, in the absence of anything to go on and probably scared out of their bullet-proof vests, the local constabulary was still "investigating."

The press had been having a field day. There was talk of an inquest, which led to rumors that the young poetess had been hopped to the eyeballs (my own personal and uncopyrighted theory), which led to innuendos that her seventh-floor aerie was a dope nest, or a love nest open to the public, or a revolutionary cell, or a whole lot else, most of it libelous if the subject had been around to sue. The track teams from the local TV stations had interviewed everybody in sight except the building janitor, who must have been holding out for a fee, and it had been front page in the *Times* every breakfast, with pictures of the scrambled corpus next to another they'd dug up of Daddy holding baby Karen high in the air, and an editorial pissing and moaning about the violence of the new generation.

The works, in short.

Well, it was a good story. While it lasted, it must have sold plenty of papers, and you could imagine the sponsors of the Six O'Clock News doing handstands.

Only now the family wanted the muzzle on.

"We represent them, of course," said George S. Curie III. "We always have, on both sides, Beydons and Diehls. Whatever you undertake to do, they're to be kept out of it insofar as possible.

"Now," he said, "it's already clear to us from the facts that Karen's death was accidental. The rest," with a wave of his hand, "is yellow journalism. The police, of course, have their duties, and obviously we can't be involved in obstructing the pursuit of justice. If there's to be a coroner's inquest, so be it, but as a practical matter we . . . Mr. Beydon . . . would prefer not. We leave it to your discretion.

"Meanwhile, we want the press called off. They've had their fun, now let them wrap up the story.

"And of course, the sooner the police close their files the better.

"How you do it, that's up to you. You'll be amply recompensed, for yourself and incurred expenses. Money's no object, within reason. I'll only repeat: We want it done fast, and we want it done . . . discreetly."

He handed me two pieces of paper, the gesture so smooth I didn't so much as spot them coming out of his jacket pocket. I glanced at them on their way into mine. One was a retainer check with yours truly as payee, the other one of those to-whom-it-may-concern open-sesame letters making (discreet) use of the Beydon name. Both were signed by George S. Curie III.

Translated, it all meant that Philip "Twink" Beydon may have loved his only daughter while she was living and grieved her dead, but maybe not enough to give a damn how she died, not enough at least to get in the way of things like free enterprise and family reputation. Which was no skin off my ass. The reporters I could handle, even their bosses if push came to shove, and as far as the law was concerned, well, maybe there is such a thing as an honest cop in California, but any time you like I'll give you my ten-minute lecture on Law Enforcement with a capital $.

According to George S. Curie III, the University would be no obstacle either. He ran through some other details—no problems, and probably you've started wondering why, if it was so easy, George S. Curie III didn't take care of it himself? I wonder too sometimes, on my way back from the bank. But then, you don't know the George S. Curie IIIs of this world. On the one hand you've got the clean-handkerchief theory to go on, and maybe at that there's more profit in wills.

Anyway, I was halfway up to my feet when it stopped being quite so easy.

"There's just one minor . . . complication," said George S. Curie III, and it was the only time he seemed to slip a little. "That is to say, before you do anything Mr. Beydon wants to talk to you first."

"Why?" I said, standing up the rest of the way.

He shrugged up at me.

"I don't know," he said. "It's his money after all, perhaps he just wants to see what he's buying? In any case I have my instructions."

He must have read my reaction because he went on drily:

"By the way, in case you didn't notice it, those two documents I gave you are both dated tomorrow. Needless to say . . ."

"You're a crafty son of a bitch," I said.

He looked up at me with that same kind of you-can't-touch-me expression he must have had on when the kids in kindergarten tried to rub his nose in it. You could call it a smile, more or less.

"He'll be expecting you at ten tomorrow morning. My secretary will give you the address."

He got up too then. The smile was gone, the gray back in his face, and old Sensible Shoes appeared from out of nowhere to show me out. She had my orders all typed in a memorandum, sergeant-major style, and she didn't even give me time to exchange names with the receptionist much less pleasantries (but I'll lay you three-to-two it was Karen) before I was standing outside again on the flagstones near the gold plaque, the heavy front door shut behind me.

I glanced at my watch—I hadn't been inside more than half an hour—and I headed for my mostly-Mustang, which all of a sudden looked a little shabby there in Rollsland, though it was only a year old, less than 25,000 miles and enough extra mustard under the hood to damn near double the speedometer.

Come to think of it, they never did ask me to stay for tea.

2

I did a little homework that night, consisting mostly of swapping Chivas Regals with Freddy Schwartz of the *Times* in a juice joint over on Santa Monica Boulevard. We're not exactly what you'd call friends, Freddy and me, for one thing he's old enough to be my grandfather, but what we've got going is better than friendship, meaning enlightened self-interest.

Except that he's a jew, Freddy's the example that proves the cliché. He's got the red nose (with mole), the rheumy eyes, the ruined liver, the soured soul, of the classic cityroom hack. Also the computerful of garbage upstairs and the unwritten Great American Novel. With Freddy Schwartz, it's all in his head. For instance, he can tell you more than you want to know about the membership of the California Club, from sex life to hemorrhoids, and this all the way back to 1940 and before. One time just for nothing he laid on me the private lives of their Excellencies, the past three governors of our sovereign state, and I told him he ought to make a Great American Novel out of it, and he looked at me crooked like I was a spy for Jacqueline Susann or somebody, then said he already had the first chapter done—in his head, of course, and then a couple of shots later would you believe the tears started rolling down his cheeks?

Anyway, for a newspaperman who pulls down maybe

a thou a month and pisses his life away within walking distance of a barstool, he's a useful little guy.

But then you could say he's got a pretty fair bunch of legmen doing his job for him, such as yours truly.

Between us we filled out a working biography of one Philip "Twink" Beydon and family, or what was left of it. Leaving out some of the more picturesque details, I came away with this:

Chapter 1: *Philip Beydon.* Born 1919 up near Sacramento. Father, a smalltown banker, had some trouble with the law but got through one bankruptcy in time for another circa 1931 and died a pretty wealthy cardiac in 1950. The first anyone ever heard of young Philip was at Berkeley in the late '30s. That's where the "Twink" came in too. If you go back that far, maybe you'll remember the Katzenjammer Kids who were supposed to do for Cal what Ernie Nevers had done for Stanford? Only it never came off? One of the reasons it never came off being that midway through his junior year Twink Beydon ran into the goal post scoring a touchdown and broke his hip. Even so he made honorable mention All-American that year, and the next year was supposed to be the Rose Bowl, with a pro contract waiting at the end. Except that Twink stumped the experts again and all the broken hearts at Sigma Chi had to go back to rooting for a bunch of stiffs whose names ended in *icz.* Meaning simply that the hero upped and got married.

End of Chapter 1.

Chapter 2: *Nancy Diehl Beydon.* According to Freddy Schwartz, it was the scandal of the season. You didn't become a Diehl by marriage, then or now, with nothing going for you but a mended hip and a fistful of press clippings, and Bryce Diehl wasn't about to make an exception for the second of his four children and only daughter. The tycoon with a heart of honey? Not this time anyway, and when the week after her twenty-first birthday Nancy came home with her name changed by act of the sovereign state of Nevada, he damned and disowned her publicly, irrevocably and eternally, or at least until the Diehl Ranch toppled into the ocean. According to Freddy Schwartz she'd been nothing if not the dutiful daughter before. She'd won her blue ribbons in the jodhpur set, she'd done the coming-out bit, had gone to the right schools and worked for the right charities. But not even Daddy and excommunication could keep her from her beloved Twink. "It was a love match if ever there was one," said Freddy, waving sentimentally to the bartender. I had some reservations of my own, but if it was peculiar that it had taken over a decade of love to spring little Karen out of the connubial nest, the thought didn't occur to me then. In any case Nancy's exile stayed in force until Bryce Diehl rejoined his Maker and her brothers came into their own, some several millions' worth give or take a hundred in such tangibles as land, oil, rolling and four-legged stock, dollars, and Oh yes, land.

End of Chapter 2.

Chapter 3 you could call: *Twink Beydon Strikes It Rich.* First he had the war to win, and a chestful of medals (sometimes I wonder if World War II medals isn't another *Mayflower* story, but no matter), and then his fortune to make, and to hear Freddy tell it it was Saturday's hero all over again, one hundred yards of green, the stripes painted gold and nobody in his way this time but a blonde number with L-O-V-E printed in diamonds across her megaphone. How did he do it? He did it with nothing, i.e., in the time-honored Western way. Maybe people in the rest of the world do it by making things, but the big California loot has come from what was already here when there was nobody but a few Indians scratching around in the dirt and fishing the rivers. Meaning the land, and what's under it—gold, oil and gas—and what grows on top—food and lumber. Meaning the surface itself, there to be carved up and flattened and subdivided and pulverized and carved up again, and also the water that runs down out of the few mountains left over after the flattening. California wealth is grabbers' wealth, where the guy with the longest reach gets the T-bone and there's still enough hamburger to feed another twenty million.

Well, Twink Beydon had a longer reach than most. According to Freddy he also had brains, guts, ambition, and I suppose it never hurt him either to let it be known whose son-in-law he was, even though he never got as close to old Bryce Diehl as the morning milkman. Anyway, at one time or another Twink's entrepreneured a few bucks out of most of the things I've mentioned and sometimes in combinations, and of course in the long run he even entrepreneured the Diehls.

That's where the story got complicated. Not even Freddy Schwartz knew all the ins and outs of it. It started and ended with the Diehl Ranch, but to tell it right you'd have to go all the way back to the original land grants when the first Diehls slickered half of Southern California away from the Spaniards, which I'm not about to do lest it stir up the Indians who owned it before. So imagine about 100,000 acres of virgin land stretching from the Pacific almost to the desert, rolling hills mostly, arid land but good for grazing, with enough orange groves where there's water to keep the whole country in Minute Maid and here and there a few small forests of oil pumps to break up the décor—and you've got the basis of what was, still is, one of the biggest California fortunes going. Bryce Diehl ran it, and two generations of Diehls before him, and after he kicked off it was his sons' turn to feed the chickens and bring in the hay.

But something came along that made all that had been look as penny ante as the original Woolworth's candy store.

The old boy must have had an inkling at that. At least he set up the organization for it: the Diehl Corporation, the Bryce Diehl Foundation, Diehl Exploitation Inc., and God-knows-what-other tax dodges. Over it all: the InterDiehl Holding Company. He did it partly, Freddy said, to beat Internal Revenue, partly to keep his son-in-law's hand out of the till. To judge, the first worked out a lot better than the second, because if today the checks of InterDiehl Holding are signed by Bryce Diehl Jr., President and Chairman of the Board, you know who's laying out the book and handing him the pen.

According to Freddy it was Nancy who brought Twink back into the fold, but you could also put it up to fate, necessity, call it greed. Which isn't to say the Diehl brothers are mental retards necessarily or that left to themselves they couldn't have developed and peddled the housing tracts, marinas, industrial parks and all the rest of the eyesores with phony Spanish names that'll keep their great-grandchildren in Sugar Frosted Flakes. But it took a five-star grabber to put it all together and come up with Diehl. That's right: Diehl. Diehl, California. The smart money says that by the turn of the century, if we ever get there, there'll be as many as 500,000 happy Americans living and working in the city of Diehl, California, and those half million are going to have to eat, sleep, shit, screw, pray, play golf, and watch TV, and die, and their children are going to have to go to school, and so on, and every night before they go to bed (it says in the Master Plan) they'll get down on their knees and thank Philip "Twink" Beydon for making their dreams come true. Oh there are still some wrinkles to be ironed out, like whether to start the little hideaways down in Diehl Cove at $75,000 or $100,000, and some politicians to be paid off, and the eco freaks and the civil rights nuts beating their breasts, but once something like that gets started out here, it takes a lot more than the Sierra Club and Huey P. Newton to plug up the dike.

Diehl, California. At that I guess it sounds better than Beydonville.

Freddy gave me the angle on some other things too. Like the Diehl Stables. If you've hung around the local horse parlors you're sure to have seen one or another of the Diehls in the winner's circle smiling at the silverware, but it took Twink Beydon to turn a profit on it. The Diehl Charities too, and Diehl Culture. Giving it away was Nancy's department, but you can bet that wherever the money went the name went with it. Discretion, my ass. And when the new football stadium goes up at the University, the same one Karen went to, what do you suppose they're going to call it?

Then Nancy Beydon up and died, of cancer, and there was just one chapter left. Call it: *The Short and Happy Life of Karen Bryce Beydon.* Freddy couldn't write it any more than I could, but he had the same theory: that the young lady thought she could fly, and it made perfect sense to him that Twink would try to get what was left of her underground and no questions asked.

"You oughta make a novel out of it," I told him. "It's a hell of a story, Freddy, and who else could tell it?"

"Do you really think . . . ?" he started. He looked up at me like a little dog trying to figure out if his master was going to give him his Yummy or take it away.

I didn't grin or anything, but then he said, "Fuck off, Cage," morosely, and he stuck his nose back in his sauce.

I patted him on the shoulder, told him to put in a

good word for me in *shul* and laid enough salad on the bartender to keep him going till closing, which sum I entered in the little spiral I use for a gyp sheet. Then I got the Mustang from the flunkey and headed west on the freeway, feeling pretty chipper on the whole. I worked off some of the Chivas Regal in the gym, which I sometimes do when the moon is up and the stiffs asleep, and the rest of it on a number from Air France who keeps the home fires burning for me now and then, and later on I dreamt I was flying out of L.A. on a Ferris wheel big enough to hold half a dozen 747s but only me aboard, spreadeagled on my belly and looking down at the world through a big bottom bubble. But then the bottom bubble was gone, there was just me making like a Sabre jet over what looked like a bunch of green waves, whooooosh, and when I woke up, it was another morning in sunny Santa Monica, Air France had taken off, and I'd just come all over my lilypink sheets.

You could say life is made up of just such simple pleasures.

3

"I'm the man from Sears," I said. "I've come for the helicopter."

The sign said Bay Isle Club—Members and Guests Only, and in case you doubted it there was a (discreet) red-and-white barrier before the entrance to the drawbridge and a sixty-year-old stormtrooper sitting next to it in a glass kiosk reading the *Playboy* centerfold with both lips.

"Honh?" he said, glancing out at me without seeing.

"The eggbeater," I said, handing him my card. "Sorry, but one of your inmates defaulted on his payments."

The happy glaze drifted south from his eyes.

"What's your business, buddy."

"Twink," I said.

"All right, let's cut out the funny stuff, if you're another of them newspaper . . ."

"Beydon," I said, gesturing at my card. "Philip Beydon. I'm expected."

He turned back into the kiosk, held the card up to his eyes, dialed a number. A minute later the barrier lifted, and he was already too busy with his playmate to see my goodby wave.

The Bay Isle Club, Members and Guests Only, was on a narrow finger of filled-in land sticking out into a manmade marina some forty miles south of L.A. The hideaways were long and narrow jobs, and the perspective fooled me at first. I mean, from the bridge you wouldn't have said super-rich, just middling garden-variety. But each house fronted on the water, each with its own lawn and dock, and backed onto a paved alley which was deserted as I drove through.

I parked in front of the Number 11 garage, a three-holer big enough for a small fire department, and walked down a path under an arched bougainvillea trellis to a high heavy wood gate with a silver B on it. Before I could even knock, the silver B swung back and a silent moon-faced aztec let me in. He was about my height but twice my width, with straight black hair scowling over his eyes and as somber as a priest getting ready for the sacrifices. He led me through a small tropical garden, where goldfish the size of footballs lounged under the lilypads of a pond, and up a path of polished redwood stumps to the entrance.

The house split in two. Behind me over the garage were the slave quarters, but up on top of them was a glass-walled glass-roofed studio which, I guessed later, was where Nancy Beydon used to darn her socks between masterpieces. The aztec led me to the main branch, also three stories, through French doors, up three marble steps and into a gallery two stories high and shadowy, which ran most of the way to Honolulu. Down the middle went one of those endless tables like in the old-fashioned novels where the host sits at one end, the hostess at the other and the hero somewhere in between, with nobody in shouting distance but a handful of ghosts. Except this one had a top of inlaid marble of the kind they don't grow this side of the Atlantic. The chairs were throne-sized with bigger ones at the ends, and there were sideboards behind them and tapestries on the walls which maybe weren't Bayeux but close enough to fool most of us peons. Here and there in the open spaces was statuary on pedestals, and cherubs grinned down at you from the gloom, and you got the feeling that whatever Hearst had left behind in the Old World, the Beydons had snapped up.

Not your taste maybe, but it's always a little impressive to see what they do with it.

Up above on the second story a balcony ran all the way around and doors led off to parts unknown, but we went through a ground-level door and down a curving flight of steps, heading for the dungeons. Then through another door and onto another balcony, where there was a hardwood floor down below, bright lights in the ceiling and two men in shorts and sneakers chasing after a hard black rubber ball with racquets in their hands.

I leave the economics to you. Take a finger of land surrounded on all sides by water and figure out what it would cost to build a regulation squash court in your basement. All I can say is that InterDiehl Holding must have been one hell of an investment if you could have bought the stock, which you couldn't at the time.

One of the players was my aztec's double, and it took me quite a while to separate them into Gomez and Garcia. Whereas Garcia's opponent, naturally, was Twink Beydon.

He looked like what you'd expect. Six foot three about, and big and chesty, but no paunch in sight. Maybe there was some gray in his hair, but it's hard to tell with us blonds. His eyes were that clear California blue, and the only thing, maybe, that gave away his age was that his face was beef red and dripping sweat. The kind of perennial jock, in sum, who's always cleaning up the trophies in the fifty-and-over meets, and everybody says it's not fair except those of us who compete in the thirties and forties.

They'd just finished a point when we came in, the ball

slamming into the tin below the line, and Beydon waved up at me.

"Hi there! Are you Cage?"

"That's right."

Motioning with his racquet: "Do you play?"

I shook my head. As it happens I do, but I'm not much for customer games.

"O.K. Be with you in a minute."

From the look of it, Garcia was playing a little customer squash himself. Or boss squash, particularly when you think of jai-alai, where any aztec can look good losing if the price is right. Beydon served, and he backed Garcia to the wall and kept him there through a couple of volleys. You could see the slice coming, so could Garcia, and there it came neatly, just above the line in the corner. Garcia just made the return by the skin of his teeth, and Beydon put the point away with a slam we could all admire. I thought it was a hell of a way for a man to work off his grief, but to each his own.

A couple of more points and the set was over.

"I'll meet you in the bar," Beydon called up with a grin, and the silent Gomez led me back the way we'd come. We went through The Gallery, up some more steps and into what looked like a ship's lounge, with comfortable chairs and a broad picture-window view of the lawn and the dock and the channel behind it. The bar was a real one too, with stools in front and Michelob on tap. Gomez disappeared, and I walked around behind and drew myself a glass, and watched about a thirty-footer making its way slowly up the channel. A few minutes later Beydon showed up again, in a gray sweatsuit, a towel wrapped around his neck, his hair wet and slicked down.

We sat in two of the chairs by the window, and after a few pleasantries about keeping in shape he got down to what I was doing there.

I'll say this for the Twink Beydons of this world, they like to lay it all out for you. Don't get me wrong. Behind those larger-than-life meat faces, those broad big-jawed grins, those clear innocent eyes and bushy blond brows and all the gladhanded I'm-just-a-country-boy-at-heart man-to-man palaver that goes along with it, they're as crooked as the next guy and maybe a little tougher—hell, they didn't get there washing blackboards for the teacher—but at least when they let you have it you know it's going to be between the eyes and not slipped up between your cheeks like a suppository. Or so I used to think, when I was an innocent young blackboard-washer myself. But in any case my way of dealing with them has always been to let them say their piece, and with an ego like Twink's, listening was no problem.

"Whatever George told you," he said, pointing his index finger at me, "forget it. He's a great lawyer, George is, the greatest, but he's as conservative as they come, a regular Milquetoast. That's why I need him. To him, a man's reputation is number one. To me, it's about number twenty. As far as I'm concerned, a man who makes no mistakes has got to be sitting on his hands. I've made a few in my time, more than a few, but I'll take the responsibility for them and no one else. And I'll tell you this much. All this, all I've built," and he made a circling gesture with his paw as though he meant to include not just the house but half of California, "is so much dirt. That's all it is, dirt. That's what it's worth to me now. The man who could give me back my wife and daughter could have it all on a platter."

He looked over his shoulder at a big formal oil portrait of what I took to be Nancy and Karen. I looked with him. The earnest way he studied it would have made you think it was the Mona Lisa at least, which it wasn't. Oh it was them all right, you could see the resemblance, the mother sitting, Karen, age circa ten, standing alongside her, but like most of those high society art jobs it had about as much life as a couple of slabs of plastic meat in a butcher's counter.

"But I guess the only one who could do that," he said softly, laughing a little, "is the Good Lord, and my connections in that direction aren't any too good."

It was corny and it got a lot cornier. Like all the rich and powerful his talk was full of "philosophy," and to hear him you'd have thought all he'd really wanted out of life was to live with his wife and daughter in a little thatched cottage by some stream where the fishing was good and electricity non-essential. He gave me his own version of Nancy and Karen, how the one was the model of womanhood and the other was going to be, how the last time he'd talked to her, which was only a week before she'd . . . but all of it flat too, like the portrait.

But then the meat-and-potatoes came back into his voice.

"I'm gonna find out what happened to her," he said.

Not "I want to" or "I want you to" but "I'm *gonna*."

"I don't believe in accidents," he went on. "You just don't fall out a window. And whatever anyone tells me, she didn't jump. I know that."

I wanted to ask him how, but he didn't need any help from me.

"I know it in my heart," he said. "She was her mother's daughter . . . and mine. There's no suicide in the family. Hell, Nancy lived her whole life like she was going to last till ninety, and that was as true the day she died as the day I met her.

"And my brother Alan," he said. "You've heard of my brother Alan?"

No, I hadn't.

"Killed in Korea," he said, and I felt my stomach

going tight. "But he died a hero's death. They gave him the Silver Star.

"Anyway," he went on, "Karie is . . . was . . . the same way. Sure she had her bad times, crises, when the world was coming to an end, but she was a battler. She was never one to lie down and say that's it.

"Sure," he said, combing his hand through his hair, "I didn't see as much of her as I should have, wanted to. She was down here at the University, and since Nancy died . . . well, I guess I've spent most of my time in town. You know how it is. But we always could talk to each other, there was none of that father-daughter Freudian crap between us. I was proud as hell of her. She had a million friends. They were always over here, she had the run of the house, no questions asked. I . . ."

He paused and stared out the window.

The thirty-footer had disappeared.

"You mean you think she was *pushed?*" I asked, like they do on TV.

He seemed hardly to have heard me. He looked down at his hands.

"I don't know," he said finally. "Maybe she got into a bad crowd over there. Don't get me wrong, I've got nothing against the kids as a whole. Radicals, hippies, if they can show us how to do a better job I'll be the first to join 'em, I'm . . ."

He stopped again.

"Shit," he said. "Shit and horseshit. Bunch of pill-poppers, living off other people's sweat and the best they can do is puke all over . . ."

His jaw had set. He looked at me hard, straight on. "A father's guilt, Cage. But what do you know about that? You're a bachelor, aren't you?"

"That's right."

"A father's guilt. The years go by, you don't want them to but they do, and you forget what counts. It's an old story. One day you wake up and realize your daughter's twenty and dead.

"Hard to believe," he said.

He sat there with it, and then he went on:

"The truth is: I didn't know her hardly at all these last years. I don't know who her friends were or what she did. I paid the bills, that's all. I had other things on my mind, business for one. She was down here, she was doing great in school, but . . . Well, beyond that all I did was pay the bills."

He ran his hand through his hair again, then wiped it across his sweatshirt.

"For all I know she was one of them. Maybe she *was* doped up, maybe . . .

"But I don't think so," he said. "No sir. Karie was too smart for that. Any more than I think she fell or jumped. I think . . ."

For a short minute back there when he was talking about the kids, he'd had me almost liking him. But then sympathy's not my strong suit when it comes to the rich and powerful, only a certain unhealthy respect.

"So you want me to find out what happened?" I asked, not liking it even as I said it. It sounded weird, like being hired to fill a hole and then dig it up again.

"I'm gonna find out," he said again. "If I was more sentimental, I'd think it was to try to make it up to her somehow, but that won't bring her back, will it? More than likely it's to find out about myself, what makes a man like me tick. A taking stock after the damage is done."

Unh-unh, I said to myself. I gave him an I for Introspection, but this was where Cage checked out.

"That's out of my league, Mr. . . ." I began.

"I know what your league is," he said sharply.

"George Curie hired you for a particular job, right? He did it because that's what I told him to do. Well, I've changed my mind. Period. That's another thing you'll find out about me: I can change my mind. You can still go ahead with that—there are others besides me involved and if keeping my daughter out of the headlines protects their interests, I'm willing to pay to protect their interests. But as far as I'm concerned, I want to know. Anything you turn up, any new fact, I want to be the one to hear it first, not the police, not anyone else. That's what I'm buying. I'm willing to pay for it too, and if the whole thing blows sky high into a scandal, I'll take the consequences."

I got up from the chair . . . in my mind. I guess it showed though, because he gave me the look that went with the worm-curling tone.

"I said I'll pay for it," he said. "Your guarantee is double what you have already, and there's more if you need it. You'll get it from me, not George. In fact I'd as soon he didn't know about it, not that I give a good goddam. I've already given my staff their instructions."

Well, it was the second time in less than twenty-four hours that somebody'd had me pegged in advance. It sort of piqued my *amour propre*, if you know what I mean. And there were other things I didn't like about it, such as his overnight change of heart and all that soul-searching in front of a perfect stranger, plus how a stiff who got caught in the middle with people like Beydon and the Diehls could get squashed like a bug and nobody to sing at his wake. Also I had that feeling in my stomach, the kind you get when you've swallowed something whole and live. Call it adrenalin, call it fear, I'm not particular, but I know it and I don't like it.

But then my *amour propre* flipped over on the other side, and I found myself thinking redblooded male thoughts, like annuities and Cage's Personal Retirement

Plan and what it would be like some day to own a piece of a Bay Isle Club myself and hang around the squash court swapping war stories with the help.

And you can call that greed, if it's easy on your ears.

In any case he wasn't the type to be kept waiting. I decided that I didn't like him any better than he did me. Or trust him, it goes without saying.

But I sat down again . . . in my mind.

He didn't have any theories for me, at least any he wanted to share. All he could do was open a few more sesames for me, like with the bigwigs at the University, and with the Diehls too. It didn't figure to him that they'd have anything for me and he said it was their interests he was trying to protect, but not so's you'd believe it. Another contradiction, it seemed, and I got the message that if I stepped on a few Diehl toes here and there, he'd be the last to suffer.

And then a funny thing happened, which surprised even me.

He'd been on his feet, giving orders like a general in his tent and the cords stiff on his neck. But then he stopped, over by the window, his back to me so I could see only the corner of his face where his jaw was working. And then his tone went all souly again, like Laurence Olivier warming up for a soliloquy on the eve of Agincourt. It was like he could look a long way backwards and forwards at the same time, or so he thought, and it didn't make much difference whether he liked the vista or not.

"There's something else you ought to know," he said. "Not that it'll make any difference, but if you're worth a damn you'll find it out anyway, and maybe it'd save you time."

He took in a long deep breath.

"I'm not her father," he said, staring out the window. "I am legally, I saw to that, but . . . Well, Nancy and I had our troubles back then. It wasn't what you'd think. She wanted a kid, we both did, but somehow or other it didn't happen. We had it checked out physically, but there was nothing wrong with either of us. It was one of those things, it happens to people. It got to her more than me. It drove her damn near wild.

"She didn't give two hoots about who it was," he said. "It could have been anyone . . ."

He broke it off then.

"Don't get any funny ideas about me," he said tightly. He turned on me. "Damn few people know about it and if I find out you've been spreading the word, that'll be something between us."

"What about the father?" I asked.

He shook his head.

"He's a long way away from here, and anybody'd have a hell of a time tracing him. I saw to that."

I bet he had.

"And Karen? Did she know?"

"Not from me, she didn't. I . . . Well, there's no undoing what never got done, is there?"

"Who else?"

"No one. No one who counts now."

"Wouldn't Curie have . . . ?"

"No. He didn't represent me then."

I put that together with something George S. III had told me and filed it away.

"What about your wife? Wouldn't she . . . ?"

He shook his head and the blond brows pulled down over his eyes.

Suddenly the air had gotten very thick. He was staring me down, waiting. Maybe waiting for me to laugh at him, or call him impotent.

I didn't.

Instead I thought of asking him why he was telling me if it was such a well-kept secret which wouldn't do me any good if I stumbled across it. Was that too father's guilt? But I thought better of that too. Discretion, you could say, had changed sides.

In any case, we got interrupted. This blonde frost came in, with oval specs and long hair tied at the nape of her neck and a tight-skirted walk which made you think of ice cubes rattling around in a glass.

The stalactite type, if you go for it.

She had a phone call for him. That's what she said. It could have been her way of telling him it was 11:30 and time for his swim to Catalina, because there was a wall phone by the bar which hadn't rung. But when I stood up to go, he told me to stick around a little while.

I did, about ten minutes' worth, with the view and the two defunct Beydon women for company. The funny ideas started then, about Korean heroes and Twink Beydon's virility and whether the father who was a long way away really was just a stud to Nancy, and how much of Nancy's itchy pants might have rubbed off on her "mother's daughter" of a daughter. In which case the artist, whoever it was, really had blown it. I thought too that there was a whole lot more behind the glimpses he'd given me of Philip "Twink" Beydon, and how if it ever all came pouring out at once I wouldn't much like to be standing in the way, not even if it meant stopping the winning touchdown.

"Do you think they're beautiful?" a voice said suddenly behind me.

It was the stalactite, at my shoulder, looking at the portrait and then at me.

"I'm Ellen Plager," she said with a smile. "What do you think of them?"

"I never met either one," I answered, "but if they were, I'd guess the artist blew it."

"Yes, she did," she said. "I think you're right."

"She?"

"The late Mrs. Beydon. It's a self-portait, at least her half of it."

"Oh," I said.

She laughed, a tinkling sound to register her little victory. She said Mr. Beydon was tied up unexpectedly and asked to be excused, but he'd expect my first progress report the next morning. I asked her what kind of woman Mrs. Beydon had been. She said she'd never met her. I asked her if she played squash, and the tinkle turned into a bell, and then she stared at me in a cool smug open-eyed way which seemed to say yes she did, but that her schedule was filled up right then, only she'd keep me in mind in case something opened up.

I went out the way I'd come in, alone, back through the belly of the whale where Twink Beydon used to bang his fist on the marble table, shouting for heirs, and the skeletons rolled around on the balcony clutching their sides. I didn't hear a sound except my own heels clicking on the tiles. Out by the entrance hall was a big smoked-glass mirror where I straightened my tie, cocked my hat, and tried on my best gumshoe leer.

Welcome to the team of Twink Beydon.

Except that I never wear a hat, and my soles are made of leather.

Gomez was looking busy in the garden when I came out.

"Hasta la vista," I called to him, but he didn't even glance up as I went out the gate.

4

The next time I actually saw him was at the funeral, but in between he was never more than two steps in back of me. Or in front. It was Big Daddy, my old platoon sergeant and Mrs. Hotchkiss in the third grade all rolled into one. It got so I could hardly go to the john. Everywhere there'd be a message for me to call him, either at Bay Isle or the big house in town up off Rossmore or the Wilshire office or a couple of phone numbers I didn't recognize. Mostly I got the stalactite first. I'd ask her how the squash was coming and she'd tinkle at me and Twink would come on, wanting to know what was happening, how I was doing, what I was doing, what so-and-so had said—with the i's dotted and the commas included.

I gave it to him too. It was no skin off my nards. In the beginning I used to wonder what was happening to Diehl, California, and a few other little projects I knew he had going if he was spending all his time on yours truly, but probably at any given moment he had a couple of dozen Cages mucking around for him out in the boondocks, and he took the one or two really hot ones and worried them like a dog in the gristle, leaving the rest for later.

I suppose I should have felt honored.

I tackled the Curie part of the job first because it was easier. In fact, don't tell George S. III but he could've saved his client my fee simply by letting time run its course. All I did was hurry it along a little and smooth out a couple of rough spots.

I started at the local constabulary. The sheriff turned out to be a worried little rooster, who kept one eye cocked on me and the other on the next election, and before I left I had him showing me pictures of his family. In between we got into his Karen Beydon file. It was fat all right, but the more I looked the less I got out of it. The event had taken place circa 3:05 on a Friday afternoon. Classes were in session, there were people all over the campus and students mixing in the mixed dorm. Nobody'd heard a thing. Nobody saw her fall. A couple of students had found her lying there just a minute later, but by the time the law came along—the campus law first—there was nothing left to do but scrape her off the pavement and mop up the splatter. They'd been through her room wall to wall, floor to ceiling, and found nothing interesting. I skimmed through a stack of photos and diagrams and depositions thick enough to paper the Administration Building and about as useful. Some people said she'd been depressed, but to hear others tell it she'd been the life of the campus. As far as her sex life went, you could take your choice all the way from nun to nympho. Here she was a radical; there she'd had nothing to do with campus politics. Her professors had no complaints about her work, her grade point average was closer to four than three, but on the other hand she'd gone tripping most of the previous spring quarter with a swain called Andrew Ford, and you couldn't help but wonder how she did it, genius or no. According to her roommate, one Robin Fletcher, she'd spent more time in the Bay Isle hideaway than in the dorm, and there was a footnote to another police dossier about a party they'd had to break up over there a few months back.

"What about the local drug scene?" I asked my friendly sheriff.

He didn't like that very much. He even managed to look hurt.

"There isn't any," he said. "All we get is stuff brought in from the outside and none of that's hard."

And even what there was, he said with a straight face, he could have controlled with a little cooperation from the University. And furthermore, though he didn't say it in so many words, with just a little cooperation from the coroner's office he'd have been as happy as anybody to stamp Accident all over the Karen Beydon case and clear his desk and go back to running hippies off his beaches.

Expenses? Zero.

Information? About the same.

The medical examiner was one of those long lean types with a practice of his own on the side and an Adam's apple the size of a Number 2 potato. Short on bedside manner but methodical as they come, and given to third-guessing his second guesses. He said they'd found some traces in her blood, not a lot, difficult to quantify from their data. He wouldn't commit himself to what it was, but I got the feeling she might have been smoking some grass with maybe an upper to sweeten her breath, not enough in any case to make her practice her Immelmanns. We swapped a few "contusions" and "intercranials" and he described exactly what happens when an object, a body for instance, falls seven stories onto asphalt, and still he couldn't make up his mind as to the probable cause of death.

I helped him out.

Expenses? Less than you'd think.

Information? Ditto.

Which left the so-called working press, and there I had an unexpected break. What happened was that the

East L.A. barrio blew up again, which it does whenever there's one of those Mexican Independence Days and the aztecs break out the firewater and start playing with matches. Before you know it half of Whittier Boulevard's up in smoke, the law joins in the celebration, push comes to shove, some cannons go off, the call goes out for stretcher-bearers and the taco stands rake it in like McDonald's on Saturday night. All this in living color too, Southern California's semi-annual war, and it sure beats the Rose Parade.

What it meant was that the TV teams headed back north, lugging their cameras with them, and overnight young Karie was shoved off the front pages of the blatts. From there it didn't take too much doing to get her back where she belonged among the dearly beloveds.

Expenses? Half in cash and the rest in promises of exclusives if and when the "real" story ever broke. In between I'd been given my first tour of the campus by the Vice Chancellor in charge of Twink Beydon's hired hand and I'd talked to the boss man himself four times over the phone.

Time elapsed? A little over twenty-four hours.

A piece of cake?

Not quite.

You'd think all this would have earned me at least a roll in the hay and a good night's sleep, wouldn't you? Out of common courtesy if nothing else?

I did, in any case, and I headed for home, but the phone was ringing before I got my front door open. It was the biddy from the answering service, with a stack of messages from you-know-who.

"Where've you been?" my friend, Miss Plager, wanted to know. "I've been trying to get you all over."

"I've been playing bumper tag on the freeways," I told her. "I'm hot and tired and I want to take a bath.

But if you can get it through, I'll have a phone installed under the dashboard."

"He's furious," she said. "He's ready to walk up one side of you and down the other."

I was trying to think up a rejoinder when he got on.

He wanted my report.

I gave it to him, chapter and verse, and even though I had more details for him than I've put down here, it sounded pretty skimpy with the words laid end to end, so I added a few embellishments.

"Don't shit me, Cage," he said. "Whatever you do, don't shit me. You save the horseshit for your other clients."

He told me he wasn't paying me to take guided tours of the University of California but to find out how his daughter died. He told me everything I'd accomplished so far he could have done himself just by picking up the telephone. And he told me some other things too, all in the King's English, with Anglo-Saxon for salt and pepper.

I hung up on him.

It was easy, all I had to do was take the receiver out of my ear and lay it in its nest. It would have been easier still to let the damn thing ring, let the answering service worry about it, stuff earplugs in my ears, tear the wires out of the wall, move back to Yakima, you name it.

Sure it would have.

The phone rang again. I let it go for three long rings.

"We must have been cut off," my friend, Miss Plager, said.

"A bad connection," I agreed.

Then he came on again, all milk. He even apologized, in his way. He said I couldn't quit on him then. I said I hadn't. He said I should try to put myself in his shoes, and so forth, and even though I knew it was just for show, well, I guess I've always been a patsie for remorseful millionaires. Then, somewhere in there, he said:

"What do you know about the Society of the Fairest Lord?"

I thought he was putting me on. No, I didn't know anything about the Society of the Fairest Lord, other than that it sounded like something Aimee Semple MacPherson might have dreamt up on a rainy day when the collections were off.

He was serious though. He said it had something to do with the kids.

"You mean the Jesus freaks?" I said.

"I don't know," he answered. "You find out."

And eventually I did.

So the next morning I moved out of Santa Monica and down the road a piece, some forty miles' worth. I checked into a motel sandwiched between the local airport and the freeway, where the soothing sound of the semis at night would drown out the couples from Illinois splashing in the heated pool. Across the road behind some handsome stands of eucalyptus was where the Diehl Ranch started. Further down began the long low sheds of "clean" industry, which was all the Diehls would let in, and then the first of the Diehl tracts hiding behind their walls, two shopping centers, and here and there the remnants of the orange groves, which let them call the tracts names like Rancho Naranja. It must have been gorgeous once, and they still hadn't ruined it altogether. In the light morning smog you could see to where the flat land ended and the pre-desert hills began, low humpy hills with elephant backs and a yellow-green fuzz which wouldn't burn brown for another few weeks. The sun was shining, it was hot enough for seersucker, and the phone at the motel hadn't started to ring yet, and yours truly was going back to school.

The campus was just at the end of the plain where the

hills started. Way off across the tracts you could see its towers squatting against the yellow-green background. It was new and big and unfinished and expensive, and as I found out, built for automobiles and not shoe leather. It took me most of the morning to track down the young lady I'd decided to begin with, only to find her just a hop and a skip from where I'd left the Mustang. Finally I tramped back across the huge green central mall, back past the Administration Building and across the concrete plaza where they still had the flags of the United States and the State of California at half mast for Karen, past the visitor's parking lot and across the entry road to the off-campus coffeehouse-saloon-and-hamburger-joint, which they called the Fish Net.

The Fish Net had an inside and an outside. The inside was dark and jammed. The stench of grease was fierce, so was the din from the jukebox. I held my nose, ordered a pitcher of beer, two glasses, and went outside where some boxwood hedges made a sort of patio and the action was quieter. Some bearded Socrateses were holding their morning kaffeeklatsch at a round table with a few admiring disciples, but beyond them, alone, I found Miss Robin Fletcher hunched over an empty mug of coffee and pretending to read *You Can't Go Home Again* by Thomas Wolfe.

Well, you've got to start somewhere.

I'd seen her face in the friendly sheriff's files, but not her feet, which were dirty and big. So for that matter was the rest of her. She was stuffed into a pair of jeans a half-dozen sizes too small. She had on one of those gypsy blouses which usually fit like blankets, and her boobies had been left to fend for themselves inside with only a neck chain for company. Her face was broad and round, a Cupid's mouth, blue eyes, but it took a while to pick out the details because her hair hung over them like a weeping willow. Maybe at that mud was its natural color, but I wouldn't have bet on it before it had been run through a laundromat three or four times.

She bit her nails, also her knuckles.

"Hi!" she said in my direction. "You lookin' for someone?"

"You, I think. Are you Robin Fletcher?"

"I think so," she said. "Why don't you pull up a chair and find out? Bring your beer, Brother."

I sat down and poured us each a glass. She shoved Wolfe aside, using the empty mug as a bookmark, and she put away half her beer in two hefty swallows, brushing her hair aside to let the glass through. Then she let out a big "Ahhh," saying:

"It never changes, does it? Same old horse piss!"

I laughed out loud, I guess because I never expected Karen Beydon's roommate to come on like a hooker from a San Pedro champagne parlor. Then I introduced myself and my business (the dodge I'd worked out with my Vice Chancellor the day before) and took out my pocket spiral for show.

She gave me a big disappointed sigh.

"Sweet Jesus Lord, not another one! For a minute there I took you for a talent scout."

"It's O.K.," I said. "You can leave out which hand she brushed her teeth with. Just tell me the dirty parts."

She giggled at that, sipped her beer and ran her fingers down the side of her hair.

"O.K.," she said, looking at me dreamily, "the dirty parts.

"Sure," she said, "somebody ought to tell all the dirty parts."

She did too, in time, but the way to get to the dirty parts turned out to be not through Karen but through Robin Fletcher. Maybe no one else had tried. All it took to get her going was my inimitable charm and another pitcher of beer along the way, plus hamburgers, two for her, plus a paper boat of french fries which she ate with her fingers, dabbing the ends into a blob of ketchup.

She came from Tulare County, Robin Fletcher did, which is up toward Fresno, which is the heart of the San Joaquin. They grow grapes up there and pretty much everything else that goes on your table. You could still hear the hick in her voice, certain words like "grand," and once when she was talking about Karie she said she was "skinny like she was standing in the shade of a Number Four wire," but she said she hadn't been home in three years except for one summer when she'd worked for "Cesar." She said she wasn't in much of a hurry either, it'd been a bad scene there, but in a wistful long-ago-and-far-away tone that made you wonder. The hooker bit was only her first mask. It was funny, but sometimes she seemed savvy way beyond her years and the next minute she came on innocent, little-girly, and the next she'd clam up and her eyes would get this glazed dreamy other-world expression, full of knowledge only Robin Fletcher had.

Maybe it was because she was a poet. So was Karen, so was each of Karen's "scenes" but one, so was just about everyone she mentioned. They had this deal there called The Writing Center, and once you got accepted into it you could spend four years writing poetry and walk away with your sheepskin. Not bad. The guy who ran it wasn't a professor exactly but a Writer-in-Residence, one Billy Gainsterne (another name out of the friendly sheriff's file), and his deal didn't sound bad either. Karie had had a scene with this Billy Gainsterne, and I gathered Robin Fletcher wanted to but hadn't made it. She pointed him out to me a few tables away, a shaggy lad in a suede vest with gray locks down to his shoulders, and her voice went up a few decibels as though she hoped he'd turn around, which he didn't. She said I ought to talk to Billy Gainsterne, just for the hell of it. She mentioned some others I ought to talk to too, including Andy Ford. Andy Ford was a Taurus, she informed me. He was the non-poet Karen had run off with, when she'd tried to bust out.

"Bust out?" I said.

"That's right. That was Karie, she was always busting out."

"Busting out of what?"

"Yeah. Like maybe that was her hangup, she didn't know what. Something. She was into things all the time. Everything she got into was a box she had to bust out of, and like every time she managed to bust out she found herself locked up again."

"Like what things?"

"I don't know. Like relationships. People, places. Situations. Everything except poetry, though maybe that got to be one too. A box, you know? Poor Karie."

I couldn't tell how to take that "poor Karie."

Then she said, "D'you read poetry?"

"A little," I said, which made it only a little lie.

"You ought to read some of hers. She was the best, but it was tight, y'know what I mean? Locked up, everything, words, images, that was Karie's poetry. But beautiful, weird kind of. Bloody. You ought to read some. I'll read you some of my own some day, when you feel like it. It's not bad either."

She said this last casually, looking halfway at me. Then the Cupid's mouth spread into a grin and she asked if I'd been over to the Bay Isle place yet. I said I'd tried but so far hadn't been able to get by the stormtrooper at the moat. "Who, Ingie?" she said and broke out laughing. They all knew "Ingie," it seemed, and also Tito and Henry Lopez, who were my two aztecs, Gomez and Garcia. According to Robin, they'd waited on Karie hand and foot, and she said she wouldn't be surprised if one or both of them had been after her—in a way which left all the suppositions in my dirty mind.

From the sound of it, there'd been times when the whole Writing Center had "busted out" and crashed at Bay Isle. When Karie felt like crashing, she said. I asked her if she'd ever run into Karie's father, and she said Twink?, no, he was always up in L.A. or some place, though she'd met Nancy Beydon there once before she died. Nancy Beydon struck her as weird, cold, though Nancy Beydon might have been a great painter if she'd ever busted out of her own box. Even a better writer, she said, giggling a little.

"What did you do over there?" I asked.

"Oh, things. We read each other's stuff."

"What else?"

"You'd have to know us to understand, Brother," she said. "It was a group. Not like encounter or anything, we were all beyond that. We were into other things, I don't know. It had a lot to do with the poems."

"Did it get pretty sexy too?"

"Yeah," she said, smiling, "sometimes it used to get pretty sexy too."

"What about drugs?"

She raised her eyebrows at me like I couldn't have been born yesterday.

"Sure," she said. "What would you expect? Did you ever know a poet who wasn't spaced out?"

Somehow I didn't want to tell her that I'd never known a poet.

"Was Karie into that?"

"Sometimes."

"Were you?"

"Well, you could say I've been there."

That sly knowing smile.

"What do you really think?" I said. "Do you think she jumped?"

She shrugged, an indifferent, I've-seen-it-all gesture. "I wasn't around. Like I hadn't seen much of her lately."

"Where were you?"

"Me? Oh, around. Places. The fuzz've got my alibi, if that's what you mean."

"But do you think she could have?"

"You mean jumped?" The Cupid's mouth made a moue. "Sure she could have. I wouldn't've put it past her. It was the kind of thing she would have done."

"You didn't tell the fuzz that."

"I didn't tell the fuzz a lot of things."

"Why me?" I said.

"You're nicer."

She was grinning at me suggestively through the willows. I grinned back at her. With the grin you could still see the little brat in the sandbox, but when the grin went away the fat stayed, pasty, and it wasn't any harder to imagine her hustling the action in Pershing Square, before they turned it into a garage. Then her face went a long way off again, soulful or what she thought was soulful, as though if she listened hard enough she could hear the angels singing behind the secrets that were Robin Fletcher's and no one else's.

"You're working for him, aren't you?" she said.

It came out halfway between a guess and a fact.

"For who?" I said.

"For who. For Twink."

I didn't say anything.

"Don't lose your cool," she said. "I won't fink on you. And I'll tell you something else I didn't tell the fuzz. He's not her old man."

The surprise came jumping out of me like a horse when the bell rings. Not the fact of it, which I already knew, but that Robin Fletcher did too.

"What does that mean?" I said.

"Just what I said. Twink's not her real father."

"Where'd you hear that? Did Karen tell you that?"

"Yeah, I guess you could say she did."

I tried another tack, but there was no prying it out of her right there and then, with the hamburger grease wafting on the air. Then she said softly:

"I could tell you some other things too, Brother, but it'd cost you."

"How much?" I asked.

"Not money, dumbie," she said, smiling, and for just a minute it wasn't as absurd as it sounds. But then she stood up, heisting the sloppy bulk that went with her, and those bare feet came out from under the table big as a bear's and no cleaner, and the idea drifted out of my head.

Maybe she saw it go.

"Never mind, Brother," she said. "I'll see you around. If you want to find me, just ask people. Got to go now."

Behind me the kaffeeklatsch had long since broken up. The terrace was deserted.

"Hey wait a minute!" I called after her. "Robin!"

She was already through a gap in the hedges.

"You forgot this!"

I waved the Wolfe at her, but all she gave me in exchange was the peace sign, and she shouted something that sounded like: "Jesus saves!" and was gone around the corner of the building.

At that she mightn't have been bad for a change, if there hadn't been so much of her.

5

I gave it all to Twink but the part about him. My self-protective instinct at work, I guess. You could chalk it up to boss psychology. I told him I thought he was on to something with his Society of the Fairest Lord but I didn't know what yet. He wanted me to see the Diehls, and I said I didn't see why. He said it wasn't for me to ask why, and I said I had some leads to check out on the campus first, and we compromised on the Diehls for the next day. I guess you could call that employee psychology, because I felt like I had him panting and holding in the clinches.

But I couldn't find Andy Ford, Karen's non-poet scene. Everybody knew him and nobody knew where he was. I found instead a passel of normal kids, normal in that they were still in a state of shock from the TV cameras, and the best I could get out of them was a run of awfuls and heavies, with a sprinkling of mind-blowings. And I found the poet laureate of the campus, this William Gainsterne in the suede vest, who wasn't shocked by anything.

I'd run a check on him through my Vice Chancellor. He'd been in some half a dozen colleges, it turned out, teaching poetry to the coeds, and the Vice Chancellor said he'd been a real catch for the campus because of his literary reputation. The Vice Chancellor said they were trying to persuade him to stay on permanently. I guess he looked the part, enough, and he talked low, batting his lashes when he laughed at his own wit, and in such a reasonable tone about his sex life with Karen it was all you could do to keep from reaching for the horsewhip.

He had nothing to hide, he said. Of course they'd been together, in the winter. It had been one of those inevitable attractions. An occupational hazard of sorts, from his point of view, but wasn't that what poetry was all about when it came down to it: a sudden flaming of sexuality? Still, he supposed he felt in some measure responsible. Maybe he'd broken it off too suddenly, even callously? Not that he'd been her first of course, there was Andy Ford for instance—did I know Andy Ford?—and others too, she'd told him all about them, and in his opinion she'd done some of her best work after their little affair, but . . . ?

Even so, he didn't believe in the suicide theory. Of course, he said, all poets toyed with the idea, but at least while their best work lay ahead, the creative urge usually won out. Eros over Thanatos, he said. And with Karen—not to belittle her of course, but between the two of us her talent was (had been) more potential than actual.

"Her talent for poetry?" I asked.

"That, yes. Also her talent for life, so to speak," he said, the lashes keeping time with his grin.

Himself, he chose murder as the cause of death, though in that, he said, he was purely a victim of his own aesthetic. He had nothing to go on. He didn't suppose it would ever come out, those things never did, but now that it had happened of course, he didn't see how he could go on with the local group. In fact he was thinking of leaving, he said, which grieved him, because he thought he was only beginning to appreciate California.

All in all, he said, it was a terrible blow.

I saw him again the next morning, at the funeral. He still had the vest on, but a tweed jacket over it and a tie held his cowboy shirt together. He looked right through me as though I marred his vista.

As California funerals go it was a pretty modest affair. There was the usual caravan of limousines on the freeway with CHPs on motorcycles opening the lanes, and the cemetery was theoretically open to the public, and there were enough flowers around the grave to build a good-sized float, but the guards outside the Diehl Ranch sign looked as if they meant business and I didn't spot a camera the last five miles. The Diehls, you see, don't belong to the Forest Lawn set. They've got their own graveyard back in the hills on a winding two-lane road, and to judge from the headstones every Diehl who'd died in over a hundred years had been planted there, including Nancy Diehl Beydon. It was a pretty place to be dead if that kind of thing's important to you: a view of the jagged mountains in the east and those low humpy hills off to the west, and not a hint of Diehl, California, from where we stood. The sunsets must've been spectacular.

I guess, though, that a funeral's the worst place in the world to judge other people's grief. Oh there were tears all right, glistening under the veil, and some handkerchiefs came out, and the stony expressions of the men, and the preacher adding heavy words of his own to those of the Lord, but I couldn't help but think there was something stagy about it, put on, like in church. Maybe it needed some keeners, a little wailing and tearing of hair, a dirge. Or a bottle or, God knows, a rock band. Instead I saw people starting to peek when the preacher's prayer went on too long, like they too wanted to check out who else was looking and who else praying.

Hell, give me a tearjerker movie any day.

The University contingent was there, my Vice Chancellor among them and a batch of kids looking young and uncomfortable. From their newspaper pictures I recognized the Diehl brothers, two of them anyway, who'd agreed to talk to me later that day, and their women and children. I saw the George S. Curies, III and IV, and maybe the partners who fitted in between, and a whole host of faceless faces who probably served the Diehl-Beydon enterprises in one capacity or another. My friend Miss Plager wore black, with gloves and a broad-brimmed hat, and Gomez and Garcia were in black suits which fitted them like sandwich boards. I tried to figure out what was going on inside their impassive heads and came up with a blank.

And there was my employer of the moment, closest to the grave and towering over the assembly, looking more stern than bereaved, his hair white where the sun hit it and yellowing in the shade. God knows what he was thinking.

And yours truly, a little to the side and behind, watching without seeing because there was no color, no sound, no movement, and nothing inside but that heavy cloudy space between the ears where I was supposed to be solving a crime. If there'd been a crime. Opinions were divided. But when they lowered Karen Beydon into the ground, I realized that I knew her less than I had reading my morning newspaper the day after she hit the pavement. Whereas if there was a murderer in that crowd, he didn't raise his hand and say, "I did it."

People began to stir. All of a sudden there was a crush toward Twink Beydon, as though everybody decided at once to get their condolence calls out of the way. If you'd only just dropped in and didn't notice the gravestones, you'd've thought he'd just won something, like an election. A lot of voices were mouthing a lot of platitudes in a lot of decibels, and I decided it was no time for me to salute and report in. Instead I turned toward the younger generation walking slowly away toward where the cars were parked, and a little apart from them, glancing my way, Sister Robin Fletcher.

She'd had a bath, at least one, and if it would have taken a scrub brush and lye soap to put her next to godliness, you could almost call her presentable. She had on one of those long figured Indian skirts, sandals underneath, and a cream-colored Mexican blouse fastened at the neck with a cameo pin. Her hair had been washed too, not that the color was any different but it glinted in the sun, and a bow at the neck held back the frizz. But there were things about her no soap and water could help. That pasty look for one. Her skin was pale, puffed, doughy—unnatural in a girl that age. Her eyes were puffy too, and bloodshot, though she hadn't seemed the type for tears, and she was staring at me with that dreamy see-through expression I'd noticed before.

"Hey!" I said to her. "Remember me? The man from *Time*? Now what's a nice girl like you doing in a place like this, I'd like to know?"

Not particularly funny, and it seemed to make no dent at all.

"You were going to read me some poems, remember?" I went on. "What's wrong with like right now?"

By way of reply she started to walk away from me. I touched her arm, but she jerked loose.

"Hey," I said, "now that's a hell of a way to treat a friend in distress."

"I didn't know you were either," she answered dully.

"All right," I said, "so I don't work for *True Confessions* or the *Ladies' Home Journal*, but you can't blame a guy for trying. We've all got to eat. Hell, what would you do in my place?"

She stopped again.

"You really want to know?" she said.

She turned to me, and now there was some glisten in her eyes which didn't come from makeup or the sun.

"Sure, why not? I'm always open to suggestions."

"O.K., she said harshly. "Then get out, Brother. Hang it up, cash it in. It's none of your business, it's got nothing to do with you."

"What's got nothing to do with me? Karen?"

"Karen, everything. The whole bit."

"Well, maybe you're right," I said, "but twenty-four hours ago you were acting like you had a whole hell of a lot more to tell, given the right circumstances. Who got to you in between? Gainsterne?"

It was a shot in the dark, and a pretty wild one to judge.

She burst out laughing.

"You're not much of a Dick Tracy, are you, Brother."

"Well," I said, "they signed me up for the part, but somewhere along the way the picture got shelved."

Which drew another laugh. At least her face worked better that way.

I touched her again, and this time she didn't jump.

"Look," I said, "couldn't we go somewhere and talk things over? Read some poems, for instance?"

She shook her head.

"I've already told you more than I'm . . ."

She hesitated.

". . . more than I should have," she finished.

"You mean, more than you're supposed to?"

Another shot in the dark.

"I mean what I said," she answered. "And about you too, Mr. Cage. Haven't enough people gotten hurt without another one getting his?"

Which was another of her opaque remarks I couldn't get her to explain.

"Who else has gotten hurt besides Karen?" I tried.

No response.

"What was it you weren't supposed to tell me? Was it what you said about Twink? Well if it was, you can forget about it, I already knew that."

Nothing again.

By this time most of the cars had already gone off to wherever it is people go after funerals. It felt pretty awkward, our just standing there, with no one for company but dead Diehls.

"All right," I said. "I guess you've got your reasons and that's good enough for me. If you change your mind though, here's where you get hold of me." I gave her a card and wrote the phone number on it. "Chances are you'll get an answering service, but the biddy there'll know where I am. Meanwhile, maybe you could save me a little trouble if you'd tell me where I can locate Andy Ford."

Only this time it struck closer to home, either that or graveyards made her cheeks shiver.

"Who, Andy?" she said in that other innocent tone.

"That's right, Andy Ford, Karie's longlost non-poet lover, you were telling me about him yesterday, remember? I wasted one whole afternoon trying to track him down and it's too nice a day to do it again."

"Where'd you look?" she said.

I gave her the rundown, which included his pad and just about the whole damn campus.

She laughed again.

"You just didn't look under the right rock," she said.

"Where's that?"

And she told me.

Anyone who's been around the California surfing scene will know where I mean. It's the best beach left for the board-and-wet-suit set that isn't government or private property, unless you're masochist enough to go for the Wedge at Newport. Not the most famous because it's small and in a hard-to-get-to cove and technically you're trespassing whenever you touch the sand, but when you can make bigger waves in your bathtub than what you'll find anywhere between Oxnard and San Diego, there the rollers will still be coming in, a long way in, as big as you want and smooth like blue silk.

The only reason I don't mention the name is that I've got a sentimental interest of my own in the trade secrets.

I thanked her for the tip. She bit at a non-existent nail and looked at me anxiously again, as though she had something to add but didn't know whether she should. Apparently she decided against it. I blew her a kiss goodby from the Mustang, and we went our separate ways.

I drove back to the motel, changed my clothes and poured myself a couple of Chivas Regals from the bottle I carry along for just such gala occasions. I'm not much of a daytime boozer, but I guess I needed to wash the taste of mourning out of my mouth. Then I headed over to the Coast Highway, stopped for gas, and drove south along what used to be one of the prettiest deserted stretches of coast anywhere. And still is, largely. And won't be, once the Diehl Corporation is finished with it.

I was feeling pretty loose—for one thing, I was going down the road of more than one happy memory—too loose in any case to pay much attention to what was going on around me. I was just moseying along, an even sixty-five, with a tape in the deck and singing at just the right off-key . . .

Which is when the bastards always jump you.

I was almost through the empty stretch and going up the first of the steep hills where the town starts. A few hills later the town ends and the coast goes wild again, then another town, and so on, clear to Baja California.

Up near the top of the hill, they'd cut the lanes down from four to two. It was a hell of a dumb idea, but there'd been some kind of roadwork going on and those orange highway cones had it marked off for you way in advance. I'd half-noticed a cream-colored van coming along like gangbusters in the outer lane, and out of reflex I opened the Mustang up a notch to give him room to tuck in behind me. Hell, no van is going to take me on a hill. But this guy had another notion and at that he must have had more than a coffee grinder underneath.

Only not enough. The driver was up too high for me to see him when he went by, but I saw the orange cones forcing him over, and I saw him swerve to cut me off. I saw curtains on his side and rear windows and I jammed on the brakes just as his ass end slammed into my left front fender north of the door.

There was an awful tearing sound like the twisted fingers of two tin forks pulled apart.

The van jumped like a goosed cat. It shimmied, danced along on two wheels and by some miracle which isn't supposed to happen, landed back on all fours and disappeared over the top of the hill, bumper stickers and all.

Whereas for me and the Mustang, we wound up in a ditch, also on all fours, our nose about two feet short of the hibiscused brick wall of another Diehl enterprise called Turquoise Estates.

6

"I don't believe in accidents," Twink Beydon had said.

Neither do I.

The motor was still turning over, and the dull ache in my forehead would take a while to turn into a full-fledged bruise. I backed out with a crunch and a spinning of rubber that didn't do the iceplant growing in the ditch any good, and I went after him.

Laguna's a picturesque little town in a freaked-out artsy-craftsy way, narrow streets winding up over the hills and houses tucked in every whichway, a lot of them perched on stilts, but I didn't do much sightseeing. Which isn't to say I wasn't on a good half of those streets in the next twenty minutes. I glimpsed him as I came over the second hill. Way down at the bottom a traffic light had stopped him. It went green just as I caught sight of him, and he disappeared down a side street into the center of town. I made the light on the yellow, veered down the side street, a second side street, a third, a fourth, burning a couple of stop signs en route and raising havoc with the Hare Krishnas on the corners. A couple of times I thought I had him, once when I was about ten cars back at a light, but each time he did the vanishing act. I went by half a dozen vans painted every hue of the rainbow, but none cream-colored. Maybe he'd done an instant paint job or maybe, like in the bankrobber movies, he'd rolled up the ramp of a moving truck and was laughing at me as I went by.

Finally I thought I had him cornered up a No Through street. I let out a whoop, squealed rubber on a curve, went up a hill, around a corner where the macadam ended in a fence on the side of a canyon, and almost ran smack into the ass end of a J. C. Penney delivery truck.

That's where I gave up.

"And I thought we were pretty good," I said to the Mustang.

The Mustang didn't answer.

I got out and lit up a Murad to calm my nerves. I admired the view, which was composed half of the rocky coast, cut into coves and inlets by the sea, and half of a good-sized accordion pleat in my left front fender. I'd been hearing an unhealthy scrunching noise on the corners, which turned out to be a piece of bent fender rubbing against the tire. This I managed to straighten out with my bare hands, which goes to show how thick they're rolling the metal in Detroit these days. I also rearranged the bumper a little. The headlights still looked crosseyed, but they and the rest of the damage could wait for the insurance company.

I drove slowly back to the Coast Highway and south again over the rollercoaster hills. The area had been built up a lot since I'd last been that way, but what hasn't, and if you didn't look too close it made you think of Monterey and points north. In any case the Pacific was never far from view, and whenever that's true in California you can't go very wrong.

The hills started to decline. A few miles further down the coast would go flat again, but I wasn't going that far. I turned off onto a narrow dirt road which seemed to go nowhere and did, past a paint-peeled No Trespassing sign belonging to a beach club long since defunct. None of this had changed, nor had the circle of dirt where the road ended and the jagged rocks began, still some seventy yards' climb down to the beach. A developer's paradise, and how the Diehl Corporation and its competitors had passed it up I've no idea.

There were maybe a dozen cars parked in the circle, but I saw only one of them. It was a cream-colored van with black curtains across the windows, California license plate ZNV 218, and a right ass end which looked like the Jolly Green Giant had tried to take a bite out of it.

A surfer was standing on the other side of it in a black wet suit, looking busy over his board. But the suit was dry, and there wasn't another soul in sight.

I got out and walked up behind him.

"Is this your heap?" I said.

"Nope."

"Whose is it, do you know?"

"Nope."

"You know, it isn't very nice to go around sideswiping people in broad daylight, particularly in a piece of shit like this."

"Like I don't know what you're talking about, Brother, this is . . . Hey, man! What the hell?"

I'd grabbed his rubber shoulder and pulled. The rest of him came up with it. He jerked loose, looking indignant, and fingered the rubber like it was 100 percent worsted.

"I don't like people calling me Brother, Brother, who aren't my brothers. I also don't like people running me off the road. Somebody's likely to get hurt."

He'd driven it all right. I'd have bet my last buck on it, and he looked like he knew I'd win. He glanced uncertainly toward the water, then at me, then at his feet.

"Are you Ford?" I said.

He fit the description more or less, him and a thousand other self-styled easy riders: the sun-bleached hair down to their shoulders, the tanned skin, the slouch, the blue I-don't-give-a-shit eyes.

"Me? No, like I'm Chrysler, man, I'm . . ."

I slapped him just once, open-handed, hard enough to bring a wince of tears out of his ducts but not enough to leave any marks on his pretty cheek.

"Hey . . . !" he started.

"I'm looking for Ford," I said. "Andy Ford. Is he down there?"

"He might be," he said, holding his cheek. "Who wants to know?"

"I'm a friend of Robin Fletcher's."

"Oh Robin, yeah, how's old Robin?" he began, but then he backed off, saying, "O.K., yeah he's down there, Brother, all you got to do is ask."

"Is that his van?"

"It might be, yeah, I dunno."

I had a yen to make a pretzel out of his rubber suit with him in it, another to take a look inside the black curtains, but I squelched both and started down the rocks to the beach.

After the buildup I've given it, it's a shame to admit it was a bad day at the cove, but so it was. The sun was glinting off the water, making all those sparkles the hopheads like to stare at, and there was a fair breeze chopping up the surface, but maybe the rollers had gone up to Santa Monica for the day. Some ten or twelve surfers were waiting it out near the breaker line like black ducks on a pond. I knew the feeling. It doesn't take as much patience as you'd think. Sometimes you could almost fall asleep out there, rocking along in the sun with your legs going slowly numb from the cold.

There were some numbers stretched out on towels on

the sand who seemed to belong to the action. They weren't a bad harem at that. Robin Fletcher, I thought, wouldn't have had much going for her in that company. I asked the pick of them to point out Ford to me, and she did, and I sat down next to her to watch his form.

He was good too. It's changed some since my day—they go in for the short boards now, which are trickier—but you can still spot the good ones. Sometimes you even know from the way they sit their boards. The others were paddling in and out, looking for a ride, and sooner or later each of them took his chance, wiping out in the quick break or just running out of wave, but he sat it out, waiting, an immobile blot of black bobbing against the horizon. Until, like it always does when you wait long enough, even on bad days, the right one came along. You could feel it coming. You saw the suck away from the beach, the long swell rolling in toward a crest, and then he was up quickly and riding by himself, shooting ahead of the froth like an arrow sprung from a bow, knees bending with it and body back like a sail, hands low and ready, feet shifting once, then looping and crisscrossing as a second wave hit him from the side to catch the new crest, and in finally, home free, to step off in the curdling foam as easy as a passenger climbing off a bus.

The last free ride in America, you could say, but the playmates were flat on their backs and there was no one to cheer but me.

Only I wasn't in an applauding mood.

He walked toward me carrying his board under his arm, and I got up. He had on an armless body shirt and the pants had been lopped off at the knees. His build was a swimmer's more than a surfer's, meaning he was long in the chest, in the arms too, but the rest of him was about as you'd figure.

His pals straggled in behind him, and they leaned

their boards against the rocks like shields. Even some of the snatch got up on their elbows.

"I want to talk to you about Karen Beydon," I said.

"Sure," he said. "O.K."

"I've never been much for talking to a crowd," I said, looking around at his private platoon. "Suppose we take a little walk along the beach."

They didn't seem to like it very much, but it was all right with him and we headed off toward the other end of the cove.

"Is that the way you always treat your guests?" I asked him.

He acted like he didn't know what I was talking about.

"That's your van up there, isn't it?"

Yeah, he said, it was.

"Well, your van took a piece out of me coming down here, damn near ran me into the ocean."

He shrugged. It didn't seem to interest him one way or the other. It was probably Chris, he said. I gathered Chris was the sentinel up in the parking circle.

"But you knew I was coming, didn't you?"

Yeah, he'd known.

"Our mutual friend, Robin Fletcher?"

Yeah, that was right.

"A nice girl, Sister Robin," I said.

He didn't answer. I remarked that the motor in his van sure didn't seem like the kind they sent out of the factories, but he didn't answer that either other than to say that he'd bought it like that from a guy. In fact he didn't answer anything more than was necessary until we got onto Karen, or rather onto him and Karen. I had the impression he had other things on his mind, but probably it was that subjects that didn't have to do with him personally didn't hold his attention.

We walked down to where the cove ended in a

scraggle of rocks, and there were long brown necklaces of kelp bashing into the rocks and drifting out again. I sat on a boulder and he sort of hunkered, doodling in the sand with a stick while he talked. Because once he got started he talked, and he talked.

I won't try to put it all down. In the first place he was dead serious about it, which I couldn't be. And in the second, you've already read it in a dozen novels, seen it in a dozen drive-ins. All you have to do is put on a used Simon & Garfunkel record and you'll get the picture.

It was the old on-the-road story, re-enacted for the 88,000th time in living color. The Great American Myth to some, the Great American Disillusion to more, but that doesn't keep thousands of kids from dreaming the dream and trying to live it. All you have to do is get out on the highway anywhere in the West to see it: kids with packs on their backs and thumbs in the air, kids carrying signs, kids riding Yamahas, kids in vans and old heaps which you'd swear couldn't make it to the next town, and sometimes don't. It's like an itch in the pants, an army on the move, and no matter that there's no place to go, in the summer they're thicker than the trees up at Big Sur, all of them coming back from someplace and headed someplace else.

Karen and Ford had done it in a certain style. It was his van and her money, and they slept in motels more than in the van. They made it as far east as St. Louis, Missouri, and as far north as Wyoming, where an old lady took a shine to them and they stayed a week in her motel somewhere near Cheyenne. And they turned her on, he said, and they fucked in the snow on a bed of pine needles one day when Karen was flying on acid. In between they amused themselves ripping off supermarkets, and once in Nebraska they'd knocked over a gas station.

All he said specifically of Karen was that she was a

good fuck, but not like you or I would say it. More the way he might have said a good surfer, a good skier, in other words an appreciation of her talent. And still, in a funny way, I got a lot sharper picture of her from him than anyone else I'd talked to, a different one too: of a wild little prickteaser of a bitch, skinny as a rail and running at the nose in the cold wind, her hair chopped off like a boy's, with a mean streak and an inheritance she could never spend her way through and a yen for something, what she didn't know and probably never would, only that her daddy's money wouldn't buy it.

Maybe all I mean to say is that once I'd known a Karen too.

All in all they were on the road together a little over a month. She'd kept a journal, he said. I asked him what had happened to it. He said he didn't know, but either he did or he had one hell of a memory for the names of places, people. But how come it had blown, I asked him, had the money tree run out of apples? No, he said, and his eyes went a little tight. It turned out, putting together what he said with what I learned later, that somewhere around the metropolis of Winnemucca, Nevada, they'd taken up with a family. A real one, as it happened, and godfearing, running all the way from the baby to the head man, in a caravan of station wagons with all their stuff in the back, and the head man was a big son of a bitch in a beard and suspenders who was leading his people to the promised land of the state of Washington. And when they split, Karen went with them. Only when the University opened in the fall, she was back.

Maybe a shrinker would say she'd gone looking for Daddy and Mommy and hadn't found them, and I'd be the last to argue with him.

"Who pushed her?" I asked him.

He shrugged, as though he accepted the idea readily enough, but either he didn't know or didn't care.

"She pissed a lot of people off," was all he said.

It got very quiet then, except for the crash and suck of the waves. Seeing that I hadn't clubbed him to death, some of his gang had gone back into the sea to try their luck, and in between us and them a troop of sandpipers were skipping at the water and darting back from the surf like they were afraid of getting their feet wet. I was trying to put a few things together in my mind, but the squiggles he'd drawn in the sand weren't much help.

"You and Robin Fletcher must go way back together," I said finally.

He'd let on along the way that he came from Visalia, which is up in Tulare County, and there aren't enough people up there yet so that the one doesn't know the other, unless the other's a grape-picker from Teotihuacan.

"Yeah," he said, "you could say that."

"Is she on the Jesus trip?"

"Yeah," with a half laugh, "I guess she still is."

I tried on the Society of the Fairest Lord for size, but he didn't flinch. On the other hand he didn't laugh either.

"Was Karen into Jesus?"

"Yeah," he said. "At one time or other she was into just about everything."

I'd heard that before, and also the answer to my next question.

"What about you?"

"I've been there," he said, and in that same tone which had made Sister Robin seem a lot older than her tender years.

It surprised me. I mean, I don't know what makes one person go looking for Jesus and another not, but he didn't seem the type any more than Sister Robin did, any more than it fit for two country kids like them to come on with battle-weary eyes like they'd seen the future and couldn't stand the sight of it.

"Did you take Karen into it?"

He looked at me like I was out of my mind. Then he laughed, the first big-hearted laugh I'd gotten out of him, also the last. But all he'd say was: "No, I didn't take Karen into it."

And that was that, or almost. We walked back along the beach, watching the non-action of the surfers, talking hardly at all. Once I asked him about his degree, what he was working toward, and he said, "I'm in no hurry," and I guess that's typical enough these days. But then when we were most of the way, he stopped and looked at me directly, a little trace of smile in his eyes, and he laid it on me:

"Listen," he said, "I've got nothing special against you, Mr. Cage, you play your game the way you have to and you take what hits you, but you give a message to the people you work for. Tell them they're not going to get what they want sending a pigeon around to do their dirty work for them, any more than the other ways they've tried. It won't cut it. We've got it and they'll get it when the time's right. We'll decide that, also the price. Meanwhile you can tell 'em to lay off. And I guess that goes for you too."

It came out flat and easy, not at all like a prepared speech but more the punchline of some other conversation we'd been carrying on the whole time, one where the words meant other words entirely.

Except that somebody had forgotten to clue me in on the code.

7

Never once but twice, they say.

I wanted to take a look inside that van, but two of Ford's spear-carriers were standing guard over it, and rather than make a ruckus I got into the Mustang and took off. I checked in with my bereaved father over at Bay Isle and gave him the five o'clock news. If Ford's message had been intended for him, he gave no sign of it over the phone. Nor did the story of his daughter's grand tour seem to faze him. Nor did my aching head. I told him I was going to see the Diehls, and he told me to report in again that night.

So I drove my beat-up Mustang back to civilization, meaning Diehl civilization, meaning what used to be the home for ailing Diehls and is now for ailing friends of the Diehls, two- and four-legged. Bryce Diehl had gone there to die, and, in memoriam you could say, the old bay-windowed building, sprawling over almost an acre of Diehl hill land, plus later improvements (like a modern double-winged inn), had become the clubhouse and bingo parlor for a retirement community of rich and aged. Almost at the front door is the first tee of an eighteen-hole golf course good enough to distract the pros one weekend every February. The houses of the inmates begin on either side of the first hole, and probably they never stop till the course runs out of green. There are no stairs of course, they ride around the paths on those little golf carts, their meals are catered at the clubhouse and delivered to the door, there's a fulltime M.D. on the staff, and so on.

I guess it beats Mrs. Cage's Nursing Home at that, although the food mightn't be as good.

But the extra added attraction, and what brought the Diehl brothers there (who after all weren't quite ready for the men in the white coats) was out the back door, where you happened onto the prettiest little horse farm this side of Lexington, Kentucky. Little, I should say, by Santa Anita standards. They've got a half-mile training track with a grass course as well as dirt, barns for over half a hundred bangtails, even a show-jumping layout. The Diehls have always kept their stock there when they're not out winning their oats, but lately it's become a moneymaker, on account of Doc Al Yuster and his miracle cures for broken-down Native Divers. If you follow the horses at all, you'll have heard of him. Time was that when a nag with a little breeding in his blood busted his sesamoid running down the homestretch, they shot him through the brain and called for the meat wagon—for humane reasons. Nowadays they take him to Doc Al Yuster—because's it's more humane, they say, but the Doc has had enough luck bringing them back to the races that there must be more to it than soft hearts and sentiment.

In all of this, of course, you could see the smooth hand of Twink Beydon, turning the watering holes of the rich into profitmakers for InterDiehl Holding. My two Diehls, Bryce Jr. and Andrew, gave me the million-dollar tour. Why I didn't know, any more than I knew where the missing brother was. By that time of day, with the sun almost gone and the hills turning purple, there were no horses on the track, but I got to meet the great veterinarian in one of the barns.

The Diehls had a lot of cordiality and they turned it

all on for yours truly. They were good-looking men in the California model, and the wear-and-tear of living off their fortune had left no marks. They were appropriately distressed about having lost their niece, no more no less, and they saved their grief for Twink in a way that made you wonder. As to the whereabouts of their brother Boyd, while we were sitting in the bar swapping horse stories and admiring the sunset, a phone call came through from him in New York City. Bryce Jr. took it. Though they talked the better part of ten minutes, all I could deduce from it was that Brother Boyd had spent that day, or several, in conference with a group of Wall Street underwriters. It only occurred to me later that Bryce Jr. could easily have disguised that part too if he'd felt like it.

To me, an underwriter is a guy who brings the grabbers together, the one to sell what he's going to grab before he's grabbed it, the other to give up his cash for a piece of it, the whole deal sanctified by the issue of fancy pieces of paper called stock certificates. Another one of those dirty jobs, in short, which is buried under swank offices and titles and for which the guy who does the laundry gets a nice percentage.

Anyway the leak, if it was a leak, surprised the hell out of me. The Diehl Corporation had always been a family swindle, the rumors of public stock offerings had always turned out to be just that. According to Freddy Schwartz there was enough Diehl cash in the till to keep the tracts growing from here to San Diego and back. Not that it could have made any difference as far as I was concerned—my personal horde is far too small to get people like the Diehls all hot and bothered—but it sure could have interested someone I knew, and who they knew I knew.

It was a leak all right.

The more so since a few minutes after Bryce Jr. hung up, Andrew Diehl said to me:

"We've been wondering—just between ourselves, and of course it won't go any further than right here—but why don't you come to work for us? I think we could make it interesting to you. After all, we're all in this together more or less. At least we're after the same thing. Instead of working at cross-purposes, why couldn't we join forces?"

"What we mean," Bryce Jr. said, "is that if you're interested, we think we could make you a very attractive proposition."

It had all been a show then, put on for my benefit, a way maybe of pointing out that their grass was at least as green as his, and maybe there was more of it.

I suppose I could have said: I don't know what it is you're looking for. I could have said: All your brother-in-law is paying me to do is find out how your niece dropped seven stories' worth of air and by the laws of gravity met her untimely death, and so far he's not getting much of a return on his investment. I could also have said: You can stick your proposition up your brotherly ass.

"By the way," I asked innocently enough, "what's going to happen to Karen's estate?"

Which, as it happened, served the same purpose.

Call it 90 percent luck and 10 percent intuition, or a legacy from beyond the grave of the Karen I'd known, but it was the answer they didn't want to hear. You could tell it not only in the twitch of their aristocratic cheeks but in the signal that dotdashed between their eyes.

"I'm . . . I'm afraid we wouldn't be the ones who could tell you that," Andrew Diehl said stiffly.

"After all," Bryce Jr. said, "the poor girl's only just been laid to rest."

And on her way to St. Peter, amen, but that hadn't kept one of them from hopping a plane to New York in the midst of their bereavement.

"But she must have left a will," I said. "Or . . ."

But, it suddenly occurred to me, why should she have? Twenty-year-old coeds didn't go around writing their wills. Then . . . ?

"I'm afraid we wouldn't know about that," Bryce Jr. said.

"But somebody would," I said. "George Curie would, for . . ."

"Mr. Curie doesn't represent us."

"Ah," I said, "but it seems to me somewhere I heard he did."

"He did," Bryce Jr. said. "He doesn't any more. We severed the relationship."

"Oh?" I said. "When was that?"

But all of a sudden the bar was closed, to me anyway. I could have hung around there till Doomsday and no one would have told me how Man o' War's great-great-great-grandson was going to run in Saturday's feature.

I got the message. I flipped them mentally for the bill, and they lost. Then we shook hands, like proper gentlemen mind you, but it was still: *on your way, buster.*

It was dark outside when I came across the parking lot. The stars were out, and a yellow California moon was climbing over the hills. The Mustang eyed me balefully. My mind was working overtime with variations on a theme: the theme being that young Karie Beydon had had something her uncles wanted, and probably my employer too though I still wasn't sure about that, and that whatever it was it had fallen into the wrong hands. Andy Ford's? The perfect setup for a shakedown, sold to the highest bidder . . . with yours truly as the unsuspecting broker? But the variations were endless. For instance: did Robin Fletcher, Karie's roommate, know about it? Or enough about it to warn me off? There was something I didn't yet believe in called the Society of the Fairest Lord, and Robin Fletcher, strange as it sounded, was queer for Jesus. But Robin Fletcher had thought I was working for Twink, while my friend on the surfboard had given me a message for more than one. The Diehls? Who meanwhile were negotiating with the Eastern money about something, or at least talking like they were? In other words: around and around and around, and through it all the unanswered question of whether Karie Beydon had come out of that window feet or head first.

It was too much for a stud with only a B.A. in Accounting, particularly since at the same time a corner of my mind had registered something else.

Never once but twice, didn't I say so?

And there they came, a pair of shining headlights following me out of the lot even before I'd made the quarter mile of eucalyptus-lined road back to the freeway. Except that it was no van this time, instead a black Pontiac Firebird with some three hundred or so horses galloping along under the hood.

I've boasted enough about what the Mustang could do. It's kind of embarrassing even now to admit that by the time I hit the freeway on-ramp, I knew she didn't have it. Maybe our little trip into the ditch had shaken up the jet propulsion, but I couldn't lose our friend in the Firebird. Which was precisely what I needed to do, because where I was going next I didn't want company.

Finally I gave it up, and settled her down in the third lane, making like I was headed back for the motel, a logical enough idea. He stayed on our ass all the way, a comfortable dozen or so car lengths back but closing the gap whenever it looked like somebody else might cut between. I waited till I saw the sign for the exit before the motel, then held my breath and gunned her all she had.

We shot across two lanes. We just missed the ass end of a Greyhound bus in the second and beat a two-sectioned Arco Supreme gas truck in the first. We rocked onto the shoulder, and off, and made the exit by a short hair.

It was a good idea and so was the execution. In the movies he and the gas truck would have lit up the skies for miles around with living-color flames. But the only break in the black night sky as I turned off the bottom of the ramp was a pair of headlights up at the top.

Lucky son of a bitch.

I found myself on a strange road in tractland, still on the Diehl Ranch, with the Firebird for company. It was unnerving as hell. I did the best thing I could under the circumstances. I took my first right, whatever it was, my first left, another right and a left, a zig and a zag for good measure, around a curve onto still another street of houses, and squealed the Mustang into the first open space I saw on the lefthand side. I jammed the brakes, cut the ignition, the lights, and hunkered down out of sight in the front seat.

I heard a motor go by once, then back the other way. Somebody's brights played across the windshield above my head. It had to be his. I figured once he'd lost sight of me in a place like that, he was screwed. A Mustang's no Ferrari after all, and he couldn't exactly stop and check out every one he passed to see who had the lucky dented fender tucked into the curb. Because by that time yours truly could have been halfway to Tijuana and laughing like a love-starved hyena.

The laugh turned out to be his, though.

I waited in the quiet and the dark, ten, fifteen minutes. I sat up and stared out at the lights of the good life, California style. A half-dozen houses, a half-dozen flickering TV screens. Then I eased the Mustang out of her slot, headlights off, and cruised around looking for another exit.

Only there wasn't any. I always thought they built those tract walls to keep people out, but it must be the other way round. I drove down one deadend after another and always there was that outer wall staring me down, a gray mass silhouetted against the sky. A hell of a place for the guilty and claustrophobic.

Finally I eased past the one entrance. I spotted the Firebird parked on the other side of the road, lights off, nose pointed back toward the freeway. He must have known, like I did, that in the other direction there was nothing between us and Palm Springs.

I went back into the tract, like I'd forgotten my rubbers or something, and parked in the same open slot past the curve. This time, if he'd spotted me, he didn't even bother to follow.

The TV sets were still on, winking at me out of the night like square blue eyes.

If Mustangs were tanks, I could have blasted down a piece of wall and made a run for it in the open country. I could have tried it on foot too, but it was a hell of a long walk to nowhere.

I could only come up with one other solution, so I took it.

8

According to the pink card, it belonged to one John R. Roland of 22 Acacia Drive. It was a nice inconspicuous Dodge Polara, the latest vintage, and when I drove it past my friend out by the entrance, brights on and the radio crooning a sweet tune, he didn't so much as pop an eyeball. I had no idea who he was, but I supposed there were worse places to spend a night, and there was a Jack-in-the-Box between him and the freeway where he could have a hamburger before closing.

I drove back onto the freeway, got off a few exits later, stopped for a pair of poached eggs and home fries with some corned beef hash tucked underneath, and drove off again. It couldn't have been much later than ten. I counted on my host not being home, but if he was, well maybe I could help him out with his long division.

When you think of where college kids live these days, you image some old condemned house with the paint peeling off the walls, leaking faucets and stopped-up heads, ten to a room and the pot smoke so thick you've got to wear a gas mask, right? Right. Well maybe up at Berkeley, but down my way there's just a bunch of commuter campuses where a few of the kids live in the dorms and the rest are left to fend for themselves. So where do they fend? So anywhere and everywhere. Your next-door neighbors could be college kids, depending on your salary and their old man's bank accounts. Particularly if you live in a place like Blue Pacific Villas.

Blue Pacific Villas was more like permanent mobile homes, with a touch of motel thrown in. The units were built out of wood so green you could almost smell the sap. There must have been a hundred of them, one-storied, in concentric circles with narrow patches in between where the iceplant ran wild, and two inner circles of garages grouped around a swimming pool the size of your dining-room table, and a clubhouse where the old folks could play cribbage and shuffleboard while they waited to die. A transient kind of place, in sum, for people who couldn't make the Diehl Ranch grade, oldies mostly, also servicemen and their wives and brats, a stray student, maybe the local mailman. The backmost units looked out on an Alpha Beta shopping center, the front ones on the Market Basket, take your choice and mighty convenient.

At that it wasn't a bad cover for a kid who had enough going on the side to make him in no hurry for his degree.

A few pairs of eyes stared yellowly at me as I drove in, but they were too close together to be human. The units were mostly dark except for the TVs, and the only other light besides the California moon was the pale green glow of the pool. All the spaces near it were empty. I parked in one and got out, taking along the trusty flashlight I found in Jack Roland's glove compartment.

When I'd been there looking for him the day before, the garage for Number 63 had been open and empty. Now it was closed with a padlock, and by shining the light through the crack at the side of the door I could make out a shape big enough to be a van.

A bad break, I figured. But I decided to save the van for later.

I tiptoed off the blacktop and down the path which led to Ford's, keeping in the shadow of the units. I didn't hear a sound except some distant motors which might have been the freeway, and an orchestra of all-girl cicadas, much closer.

Van or no, Number 63 was dark. The front door was locked and so were the glass doors which gave onto the little patio. Behind the doors, the drapes had been pulled shut, ditto around the back where some other doors opened directly onto the iceplant. I listened, but the snatches of Hawaii Five-O I caught came from the neighbors behind me.

Either he was asleep, or gone, or a mighty quiet fucker.

It wasn't hard to get in. The kitchen had one of those garbage recesses in the counter next to the sink, with a little gate-door which opened directly onto the path at ground level. Only a hook kept it shut. I jimmied the gate open far enough to get at the hook, pulled out the garbage pail and went up the well quiet as a mouse, then pulled the pail back in behind me and rehooked the gate.

I listened a minute, nothing, then played Jack Roland's flashlight slowly around the living room. It was furnished, I guess you'd say, in Blue Pacific modern: a comfortable chair, a comfortable couch, a Formica table and chairs, four plastic-covered stools by the kitchen counter, drapes and a matching beige carpet, none of it old and none of it new. The only thing which suggested the current tenant was a black-and-white poster on one wall of some number I didn't recognize except that she wasn't Angela Davis, Che Guevara's sister Jean or Mary Magdalene, take your choice.

The door to the little back hall was open and so were the three doors leading off it. One was the bathroom, the second the bedroom: a dresser, a red plastic chair, a double bed. Empty. The third was a smaller room: another dresser, a faint peculiar smell, a couch which looked like it converted into a bed . . . But when I went in I tripped over something soft and long and damn near fell on my face.

I flicked off the flashlight.

For a minute I made no sound. On the other hand, neither did the something. Then I felt around the wall for a switch, turned it on, and found myself standing almost on top of one of the Lopez brothers.

I thought it was Garcia, but it might have been Gomez. He was lying flat on his back, as still as a statue on an aztec tomb. A thin streak of hardened black blood ran out of his left eye and ended in the carpet around his ear. I bent down and, avoiding the hole in between, opened what was left of his other eye. I picked up his right hand. His arm bent at the elbow, and I let the hand go. It flopped back on the floor.

I got up again, flicked off the light switch and stood there in the dark, wishing like hell I had the boys from Five-O to give me some advice. I didn't know my way around much when it came to bodies, dead ones that is. Garcia's wasn't warm but it wasn't exactly deep-freeze either, and if his hand didn't feel like a live one, when did the rigor mortis set in? He must've been fairly fresh, no more than an hour I guessed, and maybe less.

I'd liked to have kept him company for a while. I could have tried out a few of my ideas on him—like did our mutual boss know where he was?—and maybe he'd have answered, maybe not. But if I'm not particularly squeamish about the dead, sometimes the living are another story. Whoever had done him in, I figured, had been cool enough to walk out and just leave him there for somebody else to trip over like a pair of roller skates.

Whoever had been cool enough to do that might be cool enough to come back, or send someone else in his place. Like a man with a badge.

Ford?

It could have been, but why would he have left his transportation behind?

Or it could have been someone setting up Ford.

Or me in Ford's place.

"So long, Garcia," I whispered to him. "See you around the *fronton*."

Before I left, I checked the place out, not enough to satisfy Sherlock Holmes but sufficient given the circumstances. Maybe what everyone was looking for was hidden under the floorboards, but all I found worth mentioning was a plastic Alpha Beta produce bag stuffed with a pound or so of grass back behind a stack of T-shirts in the dresser.

I went out in style—by the front door—and up the path to Jack Roland's Polara, his trusty flashlight in hand. I had every good intention of getting the hell out of there, but it seemed so quiet outside, peaceful, the moon a reassuring white way up in the sky, and nobody around but the cicadas who were laughing their clackers off at the way I was jumping at my own shadow, and then a small cicada voice inside told me I might never have another chance to satisfy my curiosity about those black curtains or the van.

I got the padlock off without a sledgehammer, an old talent of mine I hadn't had much use for lately. I rolled up the garage door and there she was, old ZNV 218 all right, with the black curtains and the bashed-in right rear.

The back panel doors were locked, but I managed them too, and in I went.

It was like every redblooded American kid's dream come true. He had just about everything in there, and then some: up behind the driver's seat a refrigerator and a two-burner cooker, a bottled gas setup to run them off and a mini-generator for electricity; a portable sink set into the wall with a water tank up above, complete with spigot; down the length of the lefthand wall a leather-covered bunk which looked like it might open out into two, and drawers underneath and dark-stained wood cabinets up above; more shallow cabinets on the other wall and under them a collapsible table; a tape and stereo hookup; even a carpet, wall-to-wall.

Hell, didn't I say he and Karen had traveled in *style?*

To top it off, the place was an unholy mess.

It looked like someone had ransacked it. Maybe someone had, else Andy Ford's mother had done all the picking up after him when he was in short pants. Clothes were flung all over the place: on the bunk, on the floor, leaking out of the drawers, a man's clothes mostly but also the kind of undies you don't find on a man south of the La Cienega art galleries. There was sand on the carpet, or what looked like sand, and papers, books, and dirty plastic dishes in the sink along with cigarette butts, remnants of food and an almost empty half-gallon jug of Gallo red. Every other inch of wall space had crap Scotch-taped to it, not just posters and empty record albums but photos, postcards, newspaper clippings, a lot of them torn and a lot hanging by one corner.

But the cabinets were another story.

The ones over the bunk contained a few dishes, plastic cups and tinware, all wedged into slots to keep them from rattling around, and a shelfful of groceries, mostly health nut stuff. Like a bottle of wheat germ and a half-full cellophane package of Crunchy Granola. Then I slid open the doors on the collapsible table side, and even the unimpressionable Cage got a shock that jumped his mouth off its hinges.

Out in the Great American countryside where the population is too scattered for stores, they used to have traveling merchants—butchers, bakers etcetera—who went from homestead to homestead peddling their wares out of the backs of trucks. For all I know they still do in places the supermarkets haven't gotten around to. Anyway, that's what this reminded me of. Not a butcher, though, or a baker. But a traveling pharmacy. A pharmacy on wheels, nothing less.

The funny thing was, most of the bottles had prescription labels pasted on, and some of them at least were what they were supposed to be. I mean, a bottle of calamine lotion turned out to be a bottle of calamine lotion. At least it smelled like it and when I shook a pink drop on the back of my hand, it dried right up and it didn't burn a hole. There were powders in addition to the liquids, and pills every color of the rainbow, all in bottles with neat labels on them, complete with Latin words that meant nothing to me and dosage instructions and the names and addresses of drugstores. For about half a second it almost had me fooled into thinking Andy Ford must have been the biggest hypochondriac in history. But then I opened up a phial of powder and licked a little, and even I in my innocence could tell it wasn't talcum.

It sure as hell wouldn't have fooled a narc, I thought, and kids who ride around in vans are supposed to be shaken down by the law at every traffic light. But then I thought of my friendly there-is-no-local-drug-scene sheriff, also his pension program, and I figured maybe Ford wasn't trying to fool anyone at all, that it was just his way of doing business. And mighty convenient out our way, door-to-door service, just bring your own spoon.

Andy Ford, mobile pharmacist. At that he ought to have painted a sign on the outside.

I shut the sliding cabinet door on my wit and almost missed it. Well, it wasn't hard to do given all the stuff on the walls, but there it was right before my nose, or at least the top half of it: a handbill of the kind old ladies pass out on tired streetcorners, and which hit the pavement even before you reach the next trash basket.

! JESUS SAVES !

said the lettering across the top, with the exclamation points at either end. Underneath it was drawn a crude stick figure of the great man on the cross. A quotation from the Book of Revelation ran across his chest.

As art it wasn't much, he didn't even look particularly worried to me, and somebody had torn the handbill diagonally across his thighs. But there was some lettering below the figure and at the bottom left corner in big type: THE SOCI before the tear, and below it MEE and below that what might have been the beginning of an address.

The good old Society of the Fairest Lord, I figured, Meetings every full moon, hymnals furnished, free milk and cookies.

I rummaged around in the débris for the missing part. I even got down on my hands and knees and poked around in the corners behind the driver's seat, between the refrigerator and the wall, thinking never once but twice and expecting maybe a cascade of ! JESUS SAVES ! handbills to come tumbling out along with A. Ford's prescription forms.

Nothing.

And then something. A sound, a quiet little sound, about as insignificant as a Mack truck making its way up Mount Whitney.

I must have been too full of love and prayer to hear them coming, and by the time I saw the headlights they were staring right up my ass. I twisted, stood up, banged my head on the van roof. I heard voices, but it was too bright to see a damn thing. I ducked and lunged and crashed out, screaming like a banshee, and about six of them met me all at once on the way down.

Or maybe there were twenty. Or maybe only one, who had a dozen pairs of arms and a baseball bat in each. One of them clubbed me in the belly and another in the small of the back. Something the size of an L.A. Ram caved in my legs and up between my ears Dizzy Gillespie was blowing "Onward Christian Soldiers" with the Heavenly Choir on the cymbals.

It was no contest. I think I must have been out before I hit the macadam.

9

I came to with the light still in my eyes, only it was the sun. I had a vague recollection of waking up sometime in the middle of the night and hearing the Chink guards bickering like mice. A familiar sound. I was cold, bone cold. The ache in my gut told me I was back home in Camp Number 5, since deep down inside I've always known that's where I'll wake up again some day.

But with the sun already high over the hills, the one fence in sight was the green spiked job which guarded the swimming pool, and the only people I saw stirring outside didn't have slanty eyes, and they were shuffling about on the terraces of Blue Pacific Villas in good old sunny California.

I was scrunched up around the steering wheel of Jack Roland's Dodge Polara. That was where they must have tucked me in. Mighty nice of them. I felt a little stiff in the joints but no more, and for a second there I was thinking I'd dreamt them too. But then I made the mistake of sitting up too fast, and the bugle started blasting again in my skull, and when I raised my hand to my forehead the muscle in my arm felt like the Peter Pain part of the commercials before the Ben-Gay showed up.

At least I was alive, though, and I sat there awhile wondering how that could be when Garcia was already on his way to Quetzalcoatl. When the news got out, if it did, the aztecs up in the barrio would start screaming their heads off about racism again. I told them to calm down, they'd made a hash out of me whereas they'd done a nice clean job on him. If my they and his they were the same they.

Then it occurred to me that one John R. Roland would have long since finished up his Crunchy Twinkies, kissed the Mrs. goodby and stepped out his front door, ready to slip on his ignition and beat his boss to the office for the 365th straight day. Then John R. Roland started screaming in my head, and I couldn't think of a way to shut him up. On the one hand I couldn't exactly drive up to 22 Acacia Drive, toss him his keys and thank him for the test drive. For one thing, I didn't have the keys. But on the other, it wouldn't have done to still be sitting there once the Polara made it onto the law's stolen-car roster.

Before I left, I stumbled over to Garage Number 63 and peeked inside. The mobile pharmacy was gone, naturally. I was tempted to check on Garcia's whereabouts, but from the stare one of the neighbors gave me as she headed up the circle of garages, I figured I'd outstayed my welcome.

So I plugged the Polara back together and drove it as far as the freeway. I parked it under a palm in front of a church. Then I pulled out my rusty thumb, and about a half hour later a northbound newspaper truck took a chance on me, and when he dropped me off I walked the rest of the way from the freeway exit, the exercise keeping my aches and pains down to a dull roar.

My friend in the Firebird was long gone, and when I finally found Acacia Drive there was no law in sight, no John R. Roland tearing his hair, no little Rolands beating the bushes for the missing family treasure. Only my beat-up Mustang, looking as ugly as I must have with her jaw bashed in that way.

I patted her on the snout, fished my keys out from the dashboard ashtray and listened to her grumble. And off we went, trading combat stories.

I went back to the motel. The morning was mostly shot. There were no messages for me, none at all, which was passing strange because all of a sudden I had a lot of people I wanted to talk to. I wasn't particular about the order. Twink Beydon would have done for a starter, and for a change I wanted his report more than he wanted mine. I mean, if he was paying me to get my nose spread all over my face, well, even a blocking back has to eat, but I wanted the plays chalked out on the blackboard with a big X across the guys I was supposed to hit.

Maybe Garcia had felt the same way.

I lay down on the bed, telling him all this in my mind and plenty more. He took it all. He was sitting by the picture window looking out at the channel, behind a big polished wood desk with nothing on it but his elbows. Their portrait was up on the wall behind him. He kept running his hand through his hair, and while I was talking young Karie walked in, not the one in the portrait but the one with the lopped-off hair and the runny nose, and she put her arm around his shoulder and stared at me.

"Now I'm going to lay it all out for you, Cage," he was saying, "clear as a picture . . ."

But before he could lay it all out for me, I fell sound asleep.

It wasn't the phone that woke me up, it was my stomach. My watch said two o'clock. I called the motel operator and asked her what time it was. "Why it's two o'clock, sir," she said cheerily, and I told her to put me onto room service.

I guess that's human gratitude for you. A couple of hours before I'd been happy as a pig in sunshine just to be alive. Now nothing would satisfy me short of a bath and a meal, both hot. I had them with a shave thrown in, also a couple of fingers of Chivas just to keep the ice cubes from making so much noise in the glass. All in all I wasn't feeling as bad as I thought I should be, which goes to show what clean living will do for you, and the only thing missing was something I'd been going without for more days and nights than I cared to count. An idea which led me, oddly enough, to my friend Miss Plager.

I got no answer at the Bay Isle hideaway, ditto at the big house in town. Maybe the help got Friday off. I tried the Wilshire office and the switchboard operator said both Mr. Beydon and Miss Plager were in conference and not to be disturbed, and I told her to cut out the crap, sweetly enough though to keep her from hanging up on me. She checked it out and came back with the news that they were down at Bay Isle. I said if they were they weren't answering the phone. She giggled nervously at that and said maybe I ought to call Pacific Telephone.

I tried Bay Isle again, letting the buzz buzz a few dozen times. I tried the various other numbers I'd used. Zero. I called the operator and let her try Bay Isle for me, and then on a hunch I got Andy Ford's Blue Pacific Villas number from directory assistance and tried it and a recorded announcement told me "This is a recorded announcement, the number you have just called has been disconnected, please check your directory or dial directory assistance," and then I dialed the campus and got through to Robin Fletcher's dormitory and was told there was no answer up in 708, and then I called my answering service and the biddy's substitute told me there were no messages for me at all. "None whatsoever, Mr. Cage," said the biddy's substitute.

A tough day for Ma Bell all around.

The one person I did reach, though it took some doing, was Freddy Schwartz. He had his buzz on for the day, and he was all ears. I asked him as casually as I could to run a check for me on the Diehl finances, not just the Diehl Corporation but the brothers as individuals. He wanted to know what was up. I wouldn't tell him, and he accepted it pretty well. I asked him if he knew anything about the dope scene down this way, and he said that was out of his beat but he'd ask around. I also tried on the Society of the Fairest Lord for size. He thought I was pulling his leg. His laugh turned into a cough, and for a minute I thought he was going to have apoplexy right on the phone. "You laughed when you killed Christ too, old buddy," I told him. Finally he agreed to check that one out too, but as I hung up I could see him shaking his head and motioning to the bartender.

Nobody followed me when I drove out of the motel. My bag was in the back seat and the receipted motel bill in my spiral, and I was heading home, home sweet home. It was spooky, kind of. I mean, for some twenty-four hours there I'd been right in the thick of it, the center of attention you could almost say, and now it was one of those don't-call-us-we'll-call-you situations.

The two stops I did make before I hit the freeway north were a waste of time. I went over to the Bay Isle Club just on a hunch. My stormtrooper at the gate had been replaced by another twice his size and half his age, but just as dumb. He told me there was no one home at Number 11, therefore he couldn't let me across. I said I had reason to believe there was and asked him to call up. He said there was no point calling up because there'd be no answer. I said maybe they were down in the squash court. He thought about that awhile. Then he said his instructions were that the house was closed and he was to let across nobody.

I suppose if I were James Bond I'd have gotten my scuba tank out of the trunk and gone for a swim, but as is I didn't feel like getting my knickers wet.

"What happened to Ingie?" I hollered at him as I started to back up. Something about him made you want to holler.

He didn't seem to know who Ingie was.

"The guy who used to work here," I shouted.

"Oh him!" he shouted back. "He's on vacation!" and from the grin that spread his ears I got the impression the vacation might be permanent.

I doubled back to the campus. There was still no answer up in 708, and the Fish Net was jammed to the gills with people I didn't know and didn't want to know. Even my Vice Chancellor had left for the weekend.

So I quit.

No Californian in his right mind, they say, would be caught dead on a freeway between four and seven of a Friday afternoon—none that is except a couple of million idiots, and me. The result being that it took the Mustang two and a half hours to make a normal hour's run, two and a half hours of stop-and-go in the smog, the more so because around the airport I had to turn off the air conditioning and open up the windows. The temperature gauge was into the red and going purple, and the Mustang had developed a catarrh I hadn't heard since Aunt Hilda died of pneumonia. As is, I just made it home before the grease monkey I go to closed up shop. He said with his workload and all he couldn't get around to the Mustang for a week, no way, and it cost me double his usual exorbitant rates to squeeze a twenty-four-hour I'll-see-what-I-can-do out of him.

I walked—walked, mind you—to the local gourmet shop and snack bar, and then home, loaded down with enough provisions to feed and water an army of Cages for the weekend, or at least two.

Two was what I had in mind.

I rode up in the elevator, juggled my bundles while I fished for the key, opened my door, turned on the lights and walked in on an uninvited guest.

He was sitting on my white leather couch, a little wimp of a guy, reading one of my *Sports Illustrateds* in the twilight. To judge, he'd been waiting some time, because there was a stack of *Sports Illustrateds* on the coffee table and he'd worked his way back to February. If I were his mother I'd have turned on a reading light for him, but I'd never seen him before. Except maybe in the dark.

He dropped the magazine when I came in, picked up a little cannon that was lying in his lap and pointed it in my direction. He motioned to me to sit down. I did, putting the bags gently on the floor.

Guns now. It had been a long time since I'd seen one—though I supposed Garcia hadn't been dropped by a spitball—and longer still since I'd had one pointed my way. I own one myself, but like Andy Ford with his grass I keep it at the bottom of a drawer.

"I guess you know why I'm here," he said. "It'd save us both a lot of trouble if you just handed it over."

"Handed what over?" I said.

He tried to look annoyed, but patience must have been a habit with him.

"The papers you picked off a certain party last night," he said. "Papers that don't belong to you. Like a dozen sheets, say, handwritten."

It didn't sound much like a will, but it could have been a journal. Or a piece of a journal.

"You've made a mistake," I said, "but take a look around if it'll make you feel better. Feel perfectly free."

"I already have," he said. Probably he had at that, but as I found out later the place was neat as a pin, and if he'd so much as helped himself to a drink of water he must have rinsed the glass.

"You could try my car," I suggested. "It's downstairs in the garage."

"I did that too," he said. He smiled a little. "While you were asleep."

I guess you can't blame a guy like that for bragging a little the once in a while he gets the chance, but he gave himself away.

"You don't by any chance pilot a black Firebird, do you?" I asked him.

He didn't answer.

Sure, it figured. And when I'd slipped him the night before, he'd gone back to the motel and waited for me to show again. A bona fide detective then, a genuine private eye, what did you know? I thought of asking him to compare bank accounts, but then I thought better of it. After all, he was the one holding the surface-to-surface, and though I doubted he'd been paid to use it I didn't much want to test him.

One thing made no sense though. The night before I'd pegged him as a Diehl employee. But if he was working for the Diehls, how had he known where I'd gone? I sure hadn't told them, and I was pretty damn positive he hadn't trailed me to Ford's. In fact I hadn't told anyone.

Or had I? Before I saw the Diehls?

Because, another thing: if Garcia had been sent there to pick up a dozen-say-handwritten sheets of paper, who'd known to send him?

I could think of only one person.

Well, maybe I had no squawk coming at that. "I'm going to find out what happened to Karen," he'd said, and maybe another way generals get to be generals is by not putting all their arrows in the same quiver. Just the same, it was a hell of a way to run a war, sending out the privates to make sure the other privates hadn't run off with the company payroll.

"Look," I said. "Putting a few things together, I come up with the funny idea you and I are working for the same chief. And if that 'certain party' you mentioned is the same one I've got in mind, that makes three of us Indians. And one of us is already dead, and another is holding a gun on the third. It makes no sense. How do we know there's not a fourth one downstairs ready to tomahawk whoever walks out the door? If you ask me, it's a hell of a way to run a wigwam."

He considered that, considered me, and then he shook his head.

"I'm not interested," he said.

So we sat there, and behind him the sky went purple and then blue again, a dark blue, with a sea mist rolling in to blot out the stars. Meanwhile the caviar I'd bought for dinner was slowly going sour on the floor. He was a patient little bastard all right. After a while he got up and put me up against the wall and searched me. According to the script I was supposed to jump him then, but it struck me that was the one sure way of making him use his artillery. And if he missed and I took it away from him, what was I supposed to do with him, mail him back to Beydon in a plain brown wrapper?

We both sat down again.

It was a standoff, pure and simple, and probably what took him so long to buy it was that he was being paid on a commission basis.

"O.K.," he said finally, "have it your way. But chances are it's going to cost you one hell of a lot more than if you handed it over right now."

"No hard feelings," I answered. "If you have to tell him something, tell him I wiped my ass with it. You can even use my telephone."

He was a very careful guy. He kept the gun handy all the way to my door, and probably while he waited for the elevator, and downstairs while he looked around for the tomahawk just in case, but I didn't follow him to see if he ducked.

10

I should have asked him to stay for dinner. As it turned out I ate alone, and that night I slept alone with my aches and pains and not so much as a dream, wet or dry, to brighten up the dawn. At first I didn't feel like company, and then when I did it was as though all the people I knew in the world had dried up and disappeared, including all my enemies ranging from 0 to 100 on the Screw Cage scale. By Saturday night I'd have settled for the biddy from the answering service, but she already had a date.

I know, I know, stories like this aren't supposed to work that way. Once the hero gets going he never stops, save for a piece of tail now and then, and a couple of days later it's all wrapped up in a bundle and everybody can turn out the light and get a good night's sleep. Be that as it may, the next thirty-six hours were a trip from nowhere to nowhere, and it got to me, and the only good thing that happened was that, lo and behold, my grease monkey showed up around six Saturday afternoon with the Mustang, fresh from the operating room and pretty as a picture.

Maybe I should have asked him too. I didn't. Instead I got drunk, blind falling-down drunk, stinko, and not up in my crow's nest either. I must have hit every watering hole from the Strip west before I let the Mustang take me home and put me to bed, and when I woke up early Sunday morning my head felt like a melon that'd gone from hard to ripe to mush to hard and was doing it again just for the hell of it.

I went down to the beach. The water was too cold to swim, and they had the yellow flag up in case anyone had ideas. I went out about a half mile to where they keep the mermaids and then back, fighting a rip tide the last hundred yards, not that the lifeguards gave a damn. I flopped on the beach and later, when the thundering herd got out of church and started trampling on my skull, I did it again. This time a couple of Andy Fords in the red underwear came sidling by in a motor launch to see if I needed help. I told them happily to stuff it, which cleared my noodle for good.

When I got home, I found a couple of pieces of mail propped up outside my door along with Sunday's *Times*. A letter and a package, and for a minute I thought the U.S. Postal Service had freaked out altogether. (I mean, *Sunday* deliveries? With a couple of hundred shopping days left till Christmas?) But the package had no stamps on it, and whoever had sent the letter had set it all up for Special Delivery and then changed his mind, because the cancel marks were missing.

I opened the letter first. It was an IBM job, typed on the stationery of Curie, Etc., Etc. & Curie of Beverly Hills, Palm Springs, Bond Street and Timbuktu. In the old days we used to call them Dear Johns, and George S. Curie III had signed this one himself.

On the instructions of his client, George S. Curie III wrote, I was herewith and immediately and forevermore relieved of my duties in the matter which mutually concerned us. My services, for which I was thanked, were no longer required. The enclosed check, George S. Curie III believed, would amply recompense me, and should I have incurred any justifiable expenses I was to submit them in writing to his office. Furthermore, any and all property in my possession belonging to his client or his client's family was to be returned to his office no later than Monday morning, and I was to consider this letter as having put me on notice of same. Finally, in closing (would you believe?) George S. Curie III hoped he would have the pleasure of working with me again on some future project!

For a minute, I confess, I had one of those you-can't-fire-me-I-quit reactions. The miserable son of a bitch, Twink Beydon, I'd had my head handed to me mucking around for him out in the trenches and he didn't even have the decency to can me in person, much less in his own name!

But only a minute, and maybe a good deal less.

Because it meant something else too. It meant I was a free agent again, Lonesome Cage riding out in his Mustang. It meant all bets were off. It meant, in short, that I was free to open up shop on my own, no checks cashed, women and children last.

Because what else did the letter prove in this Age of Equal Opportunity, except for the fact that Twink Beydon had changed his mind again?

Then I took a look at the package.

It had my name on it, nothing more. There was no return address on the outer wrapping and nothing inside to tell me who'd sent or delivered it. In a way though, you could say it came from the grave, and if it was a bomb, it was the kind that doesn't explode until you've put on your proverbial pipe and slippers and settled down by the fire for a long winter's read.

A handwritten bomb too, though parts of it could have been carved with a knife. More like two hundred pages than twelve, in two of those spiral notebooks they sell around the campuses, and all of it Karie Beydon. I guess you'd call it a journal at that, though there wasn't much by way of dates and none of the today-I-had-tea-with-Lord-Rottencrotch. Karie Beydon's journal: a journal of hate and a journal of Daddy.

It crept up on you. The first time you ran into it, about a page and a half's worth right near the beginning, you thought: well, it's the oldest of stories, all kids hate their fathers sooner or later, and sooner or later it's got to come out. But around about the second or third entry, you began to say to yourself: this kid's really hung up on her old man, and the next time: Jesus! She really *means* it! And it made you feel a little sick inside, more than a little, but not so much that you didn't find yourself skimming the in-between parts so as to get back to Twink.

She tried and convicted him of every crime on the books, you name it, and she did it with a kind of shrill mockery that belonged to someone on the other side of the menopause, not a wild little number in jeans and lopped-off hair. Sometimes she wrote about them in the third person, herself included, and it was Twink and Karen, and also Nancy, and also Twink's Silver Star brother, and someone she called Twink's whore or, later on, Margaret. But other times it was like she'd had him right there and was laying it on him, else writing him a letter: *You* did this and *You* did that. Like: "You murdered my mother as surely as if you knifed her in the heart," which later on became just a casual fact she referred to here and there: "before you murdered my mother" or "when Twink killed Nancy." A lot of it was in the form of imaginary conversations between Twink Beydon and Karen, but it was hard to tell where fact stopped and imagination took over. Like Twink's whore, this Margaret. Who the hell was Margaret? Something gave me the idea she was a made-up character, but then just before the end there was a reference to "Twink's new whore, whose name is Ellen," which took me to my longlost friend Miss Plager, which set me wondering whose place she'd taken in the squash court. I filed "Margaret" away in the back of my mind. And once near the end there was a sort of letter, or part of one, addressed to some brother she'd concocted for herself in a language that wasn't far from baby talk: "Brother Twinkie, let me tell you a thing or two about our Daddy," but by the time you were done you'd have sworn there was a Twink Beydon Jr. and, lucky lad, that his big sister had just clued him in on the more gruesome facts of life, including the one that it was Twink who'd sent their uncle Alan off to war and death.

Facts? The truth? Like I say, it was hard to tell. In places not having to do with Twink there was plenty of clinical detail, such as the description of what she called "Billy's member" (a rather puny one, it seemed, belonging to the poet laureate Mr. Gainsterne), and another letter to Twink in which she described going over the border to Ensenada for an abortion, only to tell him in the end that she'd made it all up, and in such a way that you could hear a hard cold laugh echoing back at you off the pages. But if there was nothing there that would have stood up in court, still all that hate had to have come from somewhere, and I couldn't help but think about the one missing fact that might have had something to do with it, that secret only Twink Beydon himself was supposed to know about but which Robin Fletcher, for one, hadn't made up out of thin air.

If it was that, though, she never let on in the journal. It was never "my legal father" or "my stepfather" or "my fake father." It was just Daddy Twink, loud and clear and with the blood still wet on the page.

I'll leave that part to the head-shrinkers. Probably they'd tell you all she was doing in those notebooks was trying to get his attention, and they'd tell you the same thing about her life, and also her death, and finally that all that father hate was really only love in disguise.

Which explains in a nutshell why I've always resisted the temptation to spend fifty dollars an hour to hear the same things about myself.

As for the in-between passages, she'd taken a stab at philosophy, and she wasn't much good at it for my money. The same went for some pretty murky attempts at auto-analysis. There were pages of just description, nature etcetera, some quirky drawings which weren't half bad, and others she'd written when she was stoned where the handwriting went crazy and which made no sense even when I managed to decipher some of it. On the poetry, which was dotted all through, I'll have to let the poet laureate's opinion stand. "More potential than actual," he'd said. To me it was pretty heavy stuff and forced, like she'd seen too many horror movies, full of bloodshot moons and knives, animals with bleeding eyes, sex-starved cunts, etcetera. Even there though, Daddy Twink was never far away, and in one there was even a little blind bird who kept saying: "Twink twike tweek twuck." I guess it was pretty obvious where she got her inspiration.

Like a bomb, I said. Yes, but the slow-ticking kind, the kind that never goes off but throbs dully in your brain and leaves that cold sickish tightness in your guts. I sat there holding it on the white couch, leafing back and forth through the pages, trying to put two and two together and coming up with two hundred. I could see why no father would want a last testament like that circulating—it certainly wouldn't do much for his public image—but was it enough to send people chasing after each other for? Some of them with guns and at least one dead because of it? Maybe so, I never having been a father, that I know of, but the brand of sensitivity Twink Beydon had shown me was strictly of the Arrid Extra Dry variety. As far as the Diehls went, assuming they'd had a falling out with Twink, what use could they have made of it? Whereas rather than trying to hit them up, any corner-drugstore shakedown artist with a little intelligence would have peddled it to the nearest newspaper or magazine.

This last idea crossed my mind more than once, and it wasn't respect for the dead which sent it out the other end, but something more valuable.

Like twelve handwritten pages. Twelve, not two hundred. Twelve sheets that could have been torn from the notebooks. A Karen Beydon sampler? Some pages had been torn out, you could tell it from the paper shreds still stuck inside the spirals, and except for an account of the Winnemucca adventure, her grand tour in the drugstore-on-wheels was missing entirely.

Could have been.

Or was it the other way around? Were the two hundred pages a sampler for the twelve, did the twelve tell why Karen Beydon died, and was I being set up as the agent for the purchaser? Because who besides George S. Curie III and his client would have known that I'd been "relieved of my duties"?

The phone rang.

My stomach jumped like a frog. Normally, once it's rung three times the biddy at the answering service takes over, and normally I let her. But this time I had one of those weird gut intuitions that the next person I talked to was going to be the one.

It was Freddy Schwartz.

"I've been trying to get you all morning," he grumbled at me. "Since when do you work Sundays?"

I didn't answer.

"Whatsamatter Cage, where's the repartee? Cat got your tongue? Hello? Are you there, Cage?"

"Yeah," I said, "I'm here."

He had some news for me all right, but he wouldn't let me have it till he'd worked me over a little. He must've been sober because when he's not, which is mostly, he takes what comes his way, no complaints so long as it's wet. But finally he got to the point. As far as his information went, the Diehl brothers were financially solvent and then some, but the Diehl Corporation was percolating again. Word was they were fishing for capital, only it wasn't the brothers who were making the waves. It was Twink Beydon, none other. He'd been to the banks already that week, and then just the day before one of the paper's stringers had picked up his trail out in Palm Springs. He was closeted with oil and they were still closeted, Twink Beydon and some half dozen of the biggest goo-peddlers this side of the Sheik of Araby. And the reason, though it was more speculation than fact, wasn't that the Diehl Corporation was bobsledding toward bankruptcy but that the timetable for Diehl City was going to be accelerated.

"Why?" I asked Freddy Schwartz.

"I thought you were going to tell me," he said. "You seem to have a different angle."

"I've got no angle," I said.

He started to whine then, like the jew he was. He said there was supposed to be a quid pro quo between us, but so far it had been all quo. He said he wasn't used to working one-way streets, he was a trader. He said so far all he'd gotten out of me were a lot of promises, and it was time I cashed some of them in. Etcetera. Etcetera.

Maybe I figured I was going to need every friend I had, even Freddy Schwartz. At any rate, he was the first investment I made for Cage & Cage out of the capital accumulated that last week, and not the worst either. It would be enough to keep him in booze till Yom Kippur, if he lasted that long, and with what was left over he could plant some trees in Israel.

He had nothing for me on the other questions I'd put

to him. I told him to keep listening. I asked him if he'd heard anything about an aztec who'd been gunned down under peculiar circumstances a few nights before, and he said he hadn't, that it didn't sound like much of a story. I guess it wasn't, because I never found an obit for Garcia in the *Times*, not even back in the squash section.

No sooner did I hang up than the phone rang again. It was the biddy from the answering service. While I was on, another call had come through.

"It was another one of your lady friends," she said. She had a way of saying "lady friends" that made it sound as though I was running a hundred-dollar-a-shot call girl racket.

"Her name wasn't Karen by any chance, was it?"

"Who? Oh that one! No, she hasn't called in three, four days. This was another one. She didn't leave her name. She sounded funny, I don't know . . ."

"What d'you mean, funny?"

"Funny? I don't know. *Funny*, y'know what I mean? She said it was terribly important she talk to you. She said it was about something she'd sent you, she wouldn't say what. She said she'd call back sometime. But if it was that important, why didn't she leave her name and number? And when I asked her, do you know what she did? She burst out laughing! Now what was so funny about that, I ask you?"

I told the biddy to keep listening too. If it wasn't Karen calling from the grave, suddenly I had a pretty good idea who it had been, and I figured I'd better wait it out in case she really did call back.

So I sat there. I read Karen, and I read the *Times*. I thought, and I caught a few minutes of the Dodgers on TV. Sutton was pitching. I never could see Sutton. Then I read some more of Karen, and to settle my stomach I grilled myself a steak, with some scrambled eggs and hashed browns on the side and a pint of Bass Ale to wash it down.

The way I had it pegged turned out to be part right and part wrong, but I got to see another Santa Monica sunset before the phone rang again.

11

For a bad minute I was reminded of the one time in my life I'd talked across the Pacific. You could hear the waves in her voice like it was going up and down with the sea, and I kept waiting for the operator to say, "Deposit ten million yen for the next three minutes please." Finally I figured out that she was the one who was making the waves, not the connection. In fact the connection was good, good enough to make out music in the background, and if I hadn't recognized her I'd have thought I'd freaked out altogether. Because it was a hymn of some kind, a hymn, and voices were singing it, and behind the voices was something that sounded like an organ.

But Sister Robin Fletcher was the one who was freaked out. Whatever she was on, it sent her up and down like a yo-yo. One minute she was flying and the next crying, then laughing her head off, then cooing at me in some weird imitation of a Marilyn Monroe, then climbing up one side of me and down the other because, she said, I was no better than the rest, then telling me I'd better come get her because she couldn't stand it any more. In between she had some coherent moments, but then the train slipped off the tracks again and went careening across the alfalfa.

"Hey sweet baby," she said for openers, "is that you, darlin' Cage? You get the package?"

"Yeah, I got it. Did you deliver it?"

"Friend of mine," she said. "Hey what'd you think of the poems?

"Twink twike tweek twuck," she said, "huis throughout. And now you want the rest of it, honh? You'd like the letter too, wouldn't you, you greedy little baby. Greedy little monster. You gre-heedy littu monster . . .

"Well let me tell you something, Buster," she said, and her voice jumped about an octave, "what makes you think you're the only one? D'you think you're the only one?"

"No," I said, "I don't think so."

"He doesn't think so," she said. "He doesn't think so. Well let me tell you something baby, there's a line around the block about a mile long waitin' to get it, did you know that? An' y'know what they're waitin' for? They're waitin' for Mommy, that's who.

"It's a long mother," she said, singsonging it. "Oh it's lo-o-ong, like it's real lo-o-o-o-ong . . .

"So how'm I supposed to get you up close to the titties? They're only two, Brother, two poor littu boobies, poor Mommy Robin's babies, hey did I ever tell you what their names were? Tell you what I'll do honey, jus' for you," and her voice went real low, "I'll give you a little suckie right now, right now.

"Here," she said. "Have a little. Here's Karen."

And she started to giggle.

I could hear the hymn behind her.

I tried to play it straight.

"Listen Robin," I said. "I don't know what the hell you're talking about, but I've got it and I've read it. So what's missing? A letter?"

"A letter? Hey listen to him now! A *letter?*"

The giggle went wild like a crow baying at the moon, and she started cussing me for being so dumb they ought to make me a guard at Disneyland, or such a smartass like I hadn't read it right there, something about a letter, Nancy's letter, it rang a bell but I couldn't think what, she had it all right, at least she used to, she said, and then her voice got caught in a trough between the waves and I tried to ask her who had it, did Ford have it? But that set her off again, tripping about poor baby Andy Ford, poor baby Andy Ford this and poor baby Andy Ford that, poor baby Andy Ford had gone running off with the goodies and nobody would catch him, not even Robin, but poor baby Andy Ford didn't have the biggest goodie of all did he?, so why didn't he come back, Andy Ford, she'd make it nice for him again, it'd be grand, he ought to know. And before I realized it, it wasn't me she was talking to any more, it was him head-on, the blond young stud on the surfboard, the traveling pharmacist, and she was laying it all out for him, Robin Fletcher on a platter, wailing for him, aching for him, like a torch song nobody was meant to hear, not even him, and even if the record was cracked, her voice too, it almost made me blush to listen in.

Then I could hear the hymn again.

"Cage? Are you still there Cage?"

I said I was.

"You gotta get me out of here," she said. Now her voice was flat, low. Robin's voice. "You gotta spring me, sweet baby. Come and get me Jesus, I can't stand it any more. There's some kind of terrible shit coming down on me. Whatever you want, but you better come fast. Like I'm stoned, Brother, I'm zonked, can you tell?" A little giggle, then: "Jesus God, oh I'm so stoned on Jesus God. I'm gonna crash, Cage, I can tell. It's a trap, honey, it's a big bear honey trap, it's like four walls and a roof, it's like . . .

"Hey Cage," she said, like she was waking up, "you ever been locked up in stir when they won't let you out?"

It sounded real enough, and then she started to sob and that sounded real too. I said I'd come get her. I said I'd come as fast as I could drive but she had to tell me where she was. I told her to try to get a hold of herself long enough to tell me where she was.

It was the wrong thing to say.

"Try to get a hold of myself!" she started in. "Oh and wouldn't you like to know, my darlin' man? Wouldn't you like to know? You and how many others? *Everybody* wants what Sister Robin's got, didn't I tell you? Like Brother Pablo wanted it so I gave him some of it, but then I took it back, and Brother Andy wanted it so I gave him some of it, but then I took it back, and Brother Tito . . ."

I could hear her suck air, hesitate, then let it out again.

". . . but he couldn't have it, could he? And you want it too, sweet baby, and I'd give it all to you, honest to Jesus I would, only you'd give it away, wouldn't you? So how could I take it back? 'Cause Brother Pablo wants it again, and now Brother Fitz wants it, Brother Phil, Brother Pete wants it," and she started laughing and rattling the names off so fast like the disc jockey back home who used to end up his request list saying, "and-for-all-the-gang-down-at-Eddie's-All-Night-Esso Station." Then she started to croon about somebody called Brother Pablo, it was a torch song like the first only cornier, it took me back too, years back, when I used to overhear my sister talking on the phone to some other number, comparing the swordsmen in their class at school, those endless conversations that went nowhere, and I tried to get across to her that I wasn't working for Twink Beydon any more, that I wasn't working for anybody, but by then she'd started yelling into the phone that nobody was going to get it, nobody except her Sweet Lord Jesus, she was saving it for Him, and I was thinking doubletime that the equation had changed, that all my equations had changed in a hurry, and trying so hard to break the parentheses out of the parentheses that I all but missed what came next.

She was yelling. She was yelling at *me* all right, yelling her crazy fool head off.

"I saw it, Cage!" she shouted. "Like I was there! Sweet Jesus God, I was *there!* I watched her go! Nobody pushed her! She went out on her own, an' I was too zonked to stop her!"

There was more of it, more before and more after till the cackle took over again, that godawful sound that started out a giggle and ended up like all the old crones of the world listening to Flip Wilson, with the crows and the geese and the banshees joining in. But maybe there's something like a telephone high, else I was listening too hard, because my brains started spilling over in every direction.

Like:

Nobody had seen her fall, and it might have taken a couple of minutes for them to find her, and at that the law would have taken at least five to get there, more like fifteen—plenty of time anyway for somebody to ride the elevator down and walk out, somebody so familiar that nobody would have noticed, somebody so zonked that all she knew to do was run. But the law had her alibi, didn't they? Wasn't it established that she'd been nowhere around? And they'd checked it out, hadn't they, down to the last comma, with a bunch of depositions behind it thick enough to send Sister Robin all the way to the finals of Miss Clean America? Well, but the law's been known to fuck up before, and to cover up where they've fucked up. Suppose Robin Fletcher had baked a cake for the law and suppose the law had swallowed it whole? Because the law had been all over 708, hadn't they, and come up with nothing more interesting than a drawerful of pantyhose to add to their collection? Nothing, say, like the two spiral university notebooks which happened to be staring back at me right then from my coffee table? Nothing like whatever it was Sister Robin had been lending out and taking back?

And beyond that: suppose Sister Robin hadn't been zonked at all, suppose the zonked one had been Sister Karen?

And suppose that what Sister Karen had was what Sister Robin never had had and never would, starting with money and ending somewhere around Andy Ford?

And suppose her telling me Karen went out on her own and she was too zonked to stop her was only as close as she could get to the truth?

Then all my maybes and supposes and could-have-beens and what-have-yous began to circle around like homing bees bringing in the honey, while inside the hive it was cliché time. Holey Moley, I was thinking, how did we get so fucked up, how in a million years? And where were we headed if our kids were already driving around with enough dope in their heaps to keep half a dozen generations jumping out of windows, or being pushed out? And Christ on a Bicycle, where was it going to end in a lot less years than a million when the sun showed up for the last morning?

Cage's Moral Awakening, you could call it.

"There is no local drug scene," my friendly sheriff had said, and the hip sheets'll tell you that drugs have gone the way of revolutions in the counter-culture. Like Outsville.

She'd caught up with herself, wherever that was. Her voice had dropped, and she was onto how I had to come get her again. She said she thought she'd better tell me where. Then she said she couldn't. Then she said she'd tell me, only she was too scared to tell me. Then she said if I was any good, I could find out. If I really cared, she said, I'd find out.

Then her voice fell all the way down to a whisper.

"It's cold, Cage," she said. "Sweet Jesus God, I'm so fuckin' cold."

I guess at that I could feel her shivering over the phone.

The hymn-singing was over, and it must have been sermon time because way off I could hear a male voice talking.

"Robin," I heard myself say, "why don't you bust out yourself?"

There was a pause, a long one. The preacher too had stopped. I thought I could hear her breathing, and then not that any more.

The line was dead.

12

He must have done more digging on me than any man has a right to do on another. Either that or a pretty damn smart psychologist was making his moves for him, who understood that the way to get at some guys isn't with racks or blinking lights or catheters, but just by doing nothing.

I guess I'm that kind. At least that's the track record. I mean, you can turn me wrongside up and tie my nards to a twenty-pound lead weight and chances are I'll still tell you to go fuck yourself when I come around. But if you want Cage to say uncle or sing any song you'd like to hear backwards, you just let him know you're there every so often, and waiting. You do it, say, about every five minutes for a month, and then you let up . . . for about a year.

That next week I had plenty of silent company, all except Twink himself, and his Indians didn't even try to hide. They were right out in the open. So for that matter was I. There was my little friend in the black Firebird, and another in a gunmetal Ford, and another with an elephant's nose and ears to match. Those were the ones I spotted, but even at today's prices he could have bought an army of shadows. They worked me in shifts. They were there when I went downtown to the newspaper morgue and struck out, and waiting when I came out. And when I went back to school that one last pointless time. And when I got my hair trimmed. And when I went downtown the second time and struck gold.

Sure I could have done them plenty of damage, and there were times when I could have given the Mustang a chance to redeem herself. But for the first, I figured nobody was more replaceable than a tail behind the wheel, and I was saving the second for when I really needed it.

So I let it work for me, and it did. I was a sitting duck. No matter that nobody took a shot at me, it got so I couldn't open my front door without the bomb going off in my mind. I searched the apartment every time I went in; I began to hear clicks on the telephone. And to top it off the dreams started coming back.

The Drummer dreams.

Funny thing about the Drummer dreams. It was only after I'd gotten back that they started, but then they were a long time going away. I guess they never did entirely.

Oh, you could say it worked on me all right.

Before I sent it off to a safer place, I spent more time with Karen's journal. The more I read, the more I got the feeling everything was locked up inside if I could only figure out the combinations. I found the one reference to "Nancy's letter." I'd seen it the first time through—you could hardly miss it—but it had made little impression, probably because the notebooks were full of letters written and imagined but also because, unless the time sequence was all screwed up, Nancy Beydon would already have been over two years underground.

"Nancy's letter," it read. Then: "HAPPY BIRTHDAY KAREN" in multicolored block letters that took up the rest of the page. But no more, because then she was off into some crazy fantasy about Bryce Diehl, the grandfather who'd had the nerve to die on her before she was born, and soon enough back to the father who hadn't.

I tried to see if it made any change afterward. Maybe a computer could have found something, but I didn't. It was all Karen, and if her voice got any shriller near the end, it had been shrill at the beginning too. I guess the difference between shrill and shriller is a pretty fine line.

Which left me back where I'd started from, with Robin Fletcher. It was on account of her that I made that wasted pilgrimage back to the seat of knowledge and erudition. My Vice Chancellor was there all right but not to me, and even old Pindick the Birdraper, the poet laureate Gainsterne, was less than cordial. The flags were back up to the top of the masts, the state of California as well as Old Glory, and the kids I ran into had the kind of information investigators must dream about, like: "Robin Fletcher? Naw, I haven't seen her around lately," or: "Yeah she's gotta be around somewhere, why don't you try the Fish Net?" or: "Like I told you, brother . . . Hey man, what the hell!"—this last from Andy Ford's old spear-carrier Chris, who didn't know where Robin was, or where Andy was, or even where he was once I'd turned him around a couple of times. She wasn't up in 708 either, it looked like nobody had been, and that's where the campus law found me, who escorted me from the premises.

I guess I just wasn't cut out for college life.

The local newspapers? Zero.

The friendly sheriff? He wasn't in, but the deputy he sent out to tell me got the message across loud and clear:

"Nah, you can't look at the files again, bud. The Beydon case is closed, locked up tighter than a nun's pussy. An' that's straight from the horse's mouth."

"I thought you said he wasn't in," I said to him.

"He ain't, bud. An' you ain't neither."

Zero zero zero and . . .

At that it must've been the sight of the deputy's uniform that put the idea to percolating. I mean, it may be simple once you've thought of it, but who in a century of leap years would think of asking the law for help?

Unless, that is, he had a pocketful of coin to distribute?

Which I had had from time to time in the past, and no matter that it had been someone else's coin, the IOUs were made out to me.

So the next morning I decided to cash one of them in, just on the off-chance.

The law's intelligence division downtown is one impressive setup, believe you me. They've got enough computers going to keep IBM whistling "Happy Days Are Here Again" till the year 2000, and the manpower to match. The only trouble is that if they can lay out what happened last week pretty well, next week's a big blank and even this week's pretty slapdash. Which means that the next time your house is ripped off and you wonder what's keeping the cops, you can bet your ass they're downtown punching it out on cards so's the F.B.I. can have it in time for the annual crime statistics.

What I was looking for came under S for Slapdash. "You can poke around all you want," my IOU told me, "but beyond that we can't be much help." Or, the way the clerk put it who brought me out the files: "We don't want to get mixed up with any legitimate worship."

S for Slapdash contained just about everything you'd want to know about religion here in godfearing Greater Los Angeles, in no particular order. There were leaflets, posters, photos, fact sheets, pamphlets, newspaper clippings. There were copies of I.R.S. tax returns. There were transcripts of sermons from the late, late shows. Rex Humbard was there, so was Kathie Kuhlmann, the

Maharaj Ji, Garner Ted Armstrong, the Ramakrishna Society, the Mormon Tabernacle, the Verdugo Hills Sunrise Circle, the original cast of *Jesus Christ Superstar*, the Masonic Temple, and some Jewish Defense League items thrown in for the ecumenically minded. Well, like everybody knows, Greater Los Angeles has always been freaked out for God, but God'll have to give the computers a hand when they get around to that collection else they'll blow all the fuses from here to the Pearly Gates and back.

In any case it was there, poking around in that holy stew, that I finally came up with the Society of the Fairest Lord.

To judge, it had had a pretty checkered history. There were no dates to help me out, but you could guess a chronology of sorts from the yellowing of the handbills. In the end I'd found about twenty of these, and I laid them out side by side on the desk I was working at, and I played solitaire with them till I got them into a more-or-less order.

The headings were all the same—! JESUS SAVES !, with the double exclamation point and the same happy-go-lucky stick-figure Christ hanging on the cross—but underneath there'd been some changes, mostly in the addresses. They were all Los Angeles, which helped explain why I'd come up empty-handed south of the county line, but up until lately they'd done a good deal of moving around. Two steps ahead of the law maybe, but more likely two steps ahead of the rent-collector. The most recent ones, though, were identical. There were meetings every Wednesday and Sunday evenings, "Bring Faith Bring Money" they said, and the address was down off South San Pedro in what I knew to be one of the less savory neighborhoods of our Fairest Lord's metropolis.

This was a Thursday. My first impulse was to rush

right over there on my white horse and save Sister Robin from the fairy dragon. But then the vizor fell down and I decided to cool it. For one thing, if she'd lasted four days another three wouldn't kill her. For another, when I went to get her I wanted to be sure of finding her, and I didn't want an escort. So I settled for Sunday, O.K. and amen, put the handbills back into the mess and returned the boxes of files to the clerk. He asked me if I'd found what I was looking for. "Nah," I said, "I guess it's pretty hopeless," and I left him shaking his head and went back out into the world to spread the good tidings to . . .

To no one.

Because meanwhile it had gotten very quiet again. Quiet enough, you could say, to hear the clicks in a telephone. I spoke to Freddy Schwartz a couple of times—by public phone—but it was more for his company, such as it was, because he had nothing to add to what had already been printed in his sheet. Back at the beginning of the week the *Times* had been full of that kind of gossipy innuendo-y emptiness which builds circulation and generally titillates the reading public. Like on Monday the columnist Freddy Schwartz hustled for published an item: "What bereaved father-about-town is about to close the biggest deal (no pun intended) of his superdeal life?" and back on the financial page was one of those superindignant pieces reporters file when they can't get near the real story, all about how the public had the Securities and Exchange Commission to protect it against the wheelings and dealings of publicly held corporations, but how about the private ones, some of which could swallow the others without so much as chewing? The message being simply that the Diehl Corporations of this world ought to watch their step, or at least be a little more gracious toward the working press. By Tuesday the insiders were stirring around on the Pacific Exchange, and out of sheer coincidence the Wednesday *Times* ran an "in-depth" story on the city of Diehl, the problems confronting it, political, financial, ecological, sociological and you-name-it-ogical, and all about as edifying as you might expect except for the "informed" supposition that, even given the great resources of the Diehl Corporation, the inflationary trend might force outside financing if the timetable was to be kept.

Or advanced?

But as to whatever the Diehl brothers might have been doing in the meantime, not a word, and by Thursday, nothing at all.

The same on Friday.

And nobody asking me about any-and-all property in my possession either, even though I no longer had it.

Very quiet, like I say. Too quiet. I felt it all around, the prickle on my skin, the nerves jumping in my stomach, like Twink's Indians had moved inside and set up shop. Oh yes, he got to me all right, and if it's too much to imagine the whole city of L.A. stopping in its tracks and holding its breath, still you got the funny feeling somebody was waiting for somebody else to drop the other shoe.

And so on Saturday, being me, I dropped it.

13

I woke up drenched in sweat and I was cold, bone shivering cold. My goddam teeth were chattering. The pillow was wadded into a ball where I'd been hugging it, the covers had tied themselves into knots down around my ankles and the California sun shining in my windows looked about a million light-years off and then some. I'd been dreaming the Drummer dream all right, but this time Twink Beydon was mixed up in it, sitting back of that same desk, the one the Chinks of Camp Number 5 must have swiped off the Russians because it was big and old, anomalous as hell, and you could picture Napoleon signing a peace treaty at it, and his goddam daughter—I mean, you try sleeping with a corpse sometime and see what it does for your night life, and . . .

I forget the rest. Or put it this way: I don't forget the rest. It's another story, for another day. The part that fits here is what I felt when I woke up with my teeth doubletiming in place: the panic, that godawful longing in the pit of your stomach for something that wasn't any more and probably never was, and at the bottom of it all that rage which made you the colder the hotter it got, like an igloo with a fire roaring inside and no way to put it out, no way Brother. Revenge, call it. The only difference was that when I used to wake up that way, the Drummer was some eight thousand miles long gone, beyond my reach, and I could eat my revenge for breakfast with milk and sugar on top. But this time he wasn't that far, no sir, not that far at all.

I did it the way experience had taught me: that is, around the end. It may not have been the most heroic, but the Drummer, you could say, had taught me all I'll ever need to know about heroics.

I'd tracked her down by late morning, my onetime friend Miss Ellen Plager. As to where, if I'd felt cute I could ask you to guess: like where do the Ellen Plagers of this world go on a Saturday morning in May when the sun's out and their boss and master is incommunicado? But I didn't feel cute. It was in a beauty parlor off Wilshire in Beverly Hills, one of those joints so fancy they call themselves something else, I forget what. It was red plush, with chandeliers overhead and fake gaslight and gilt-framed mirrors on the red plush walls, Twink's whore's kind of place, and a bunch of pansies running around in bell bottoms and frilly shirts open to their navels playing let's cut Mommy's hair.

From their expressions when I busted in, they must have thought I was out to liquidate the Gay Liberation Front all by myself. They backed up for me, tripping over their livery. I went down a line of numbers plugged into those oversized helmets. She saw me coming even without her specs. She flinched a little, and then she gave me one of those open-eyed squash-court smiles, and I grabbed her by the wrist, and out she came from under. Her head was covered with curlers about the size of rolling pins, a hair net on top, and she looked like unholy hell.

I guess you'd have to say the beauty parlor is the biggest equalizer of them all for the fairer sex.

Her smile went away.

I dragged her out toward the front door, and it went away further. The row of heads craned and gawked. I heard a falsetto warble: "Wally darling, hadn't you better call the police?"

"Where is he?" I said. "I want to talk."

"It w-wouldn't do you any good," she stammered. "He'll only see you when you're ready to . . ."

"Sure," I said. "I know."

Then: "Where's Margaret?"

It set off a race in her face between surprise, anger and ignorance. Ignorance came home dead last.

"Who?" she said.

"Ow!" she said.

With one hand I opened the door and with the other I pulled her toward it.

She went strong, panic-strong. Her eyes bulged, and the blue started to run out of them.

"Let's go," I said.

"I can't! *Not like this!*"

"Out!" I said.

She grabbed for her head. I yanked, and some of her bric-a-brac came loose.

"All right!" she shouted. "Goddam you, I'll tell you! Just let go of me for God's sake!"

I let go, stepped inside the door and closed it. The pansies were running every whichway like somebody'd let loose a basket of mice, and Wally darling was dialing a number on an ormolu phone.

"You won't find him there anyway," she said, rubbing at her wrist. "He never goes there any more."

She couldn't resist a little gleam of triumph.

"Never?" I said.

For an answer she just glared at me.

"Where is she?" I asked again.

She told me the address. It was out in the Valley, and she made sure I knew it was out in the Valley with all the smugness she could muster.

"And what's her last name?"

It brought her cool back in a hurry. She must've realized she'd been had, and all because women put curlers in their hair. It made her mad, then it made her tinkle.

I didn't get it at all.

"You know, Cage, he could kill you for messing around in this."

Then she smiled at me, the smug cool smile which was the same one she'd worn with the oval specs when her hair was down.

I saved my repartee for another time.

"O.K.," I persisted, "what's her last name?"

"You could always try Beydon," she answered calmly.

I have to hand it to her: it sent me out of there with my mind twisted into a ball. She watched me go, and Wally darling was lisping at the police presumably, and I'd given them all something to wag their tongues over till Clairol came out with a new rinse. Of course I'd been brainstorming with "Where's Margaret." "Twink's whore," Karen had called her, and I'd figured Twink's latest whore might just know something. But *Beydon!* That blew my mind inside out. Ellen Plager hadn't had to tell me that yet she had, and probably in hindsight it was her own way of getting even. But what did it mean? Unless Twink Beydon was a common garden-variety bigamist?

He wasn't, but on the spot, simple as it was, I missed the explanation. All I could picture was Ellen Plager yanking the blower loose from Wally darling and getting onto the Chief, and the Chief getting onto his Indians, and the Indians onto me. I headed west on Wilshire. When I hit the freeway I was doing sixty, and eighty-five by the top of the Sepulveda Pass, which was as fast as I dared at Saturday noon with all my fellow citizens on their way to the Akron or the Broadway or Bullock's, depending on their pocketbooks, and the highway law making sure they got there in one piece.

My escort stayed with me all the way, just the one (the guy in the gunmetal Ford happened to be the man on duty), and there wasn't any roadblock waiting for me coming down the pass, or when I switched over to the Ventura, or when a dozen or so exits later I got off. By that time my adrenalin had eased up and the Mustang's too.

The Valley, you know. L.A. is surrounded by valleys, but there's only one Valley, and to everybody who lives on the other side of the hills from it, it's a standing joke. All the same, a couple of million people manage to get along out there, and nobody's forcing them to stay. They keep their spades and aztecs penned up in Pacoima and San Fernando, and they vote Reagan, and when the smog comes on strong and the heat they lock their doors, turn on the air conditioning and wait for the next santa ana to blow it away. Sure it's not as picturesque as it used to be but what is? I guess all I mean to say is that it gripes my ass when the smart money in Mansonland starts laughing at the Valley. They ought to open their eyes and look out their own picture window.

End of lecture.

Where I went was an older section, even though it was way out near the western rim. The houses were older too, further apart and two-storied, and some even had lawns growing in front and mailboxes near the sidewalks and tall pepper trees bordering the gutters. All clean as a whistle, neat and trim, the kind of rare community where you still see kids on roller skates and people don't lock their doors every time they go out. I found my street, my house, parked at the curb, and the gunmetal Ford ducked into a space back near the corner. The name was Beydon all right, but Twink wasn't on hand to greet me, and the only reception committee was a kid, maybe seventeen or eighteen, backing a VW fastback out the driveway. He stared at me a minute as I went up the walk, then drove away.

"Mrs. Beydon?" I said, gagging a little mentally over the name.

"Yes?"

Twink's whore then, in the flesh.

You think "Twink's whore" and what do you see? Some number about as enormous as the Statue of Liberty with twice the tits. You see hair flowing down to her navel and nothing underneath it but "Mine All Mine" scrawled in red, white and blue finger paint. You see boots halfway up her thighs and around in back "Twink's" tattooed on one cheek and "Whore" across the other.

At least I did. Maybe by tuning down my imagination a little I'd have settled for Ellen Plager or thereabouts. But not Margaret Beydon in any case.

She was a short dark-eyed woman on the chubby side, with a curious ferret-like expression people might have called cute once, but which had gained in character once the wrinkles caught up with it. I put her in her late forties. The gray did her short black hair no harm, and she hadn't tried to disguise it. Legs on the stumpy side, a maroon figured skirt, a white short-sleeved blouse that pulled in tight under an ample bosom. Not bad, in short, and somehow you got the feeling she could have been better than not bad if she worked at it. But still: Twink's whore?

Yet that was what she turned out to be, at least by the prevailing moralities.

Something told me to play it straight with her and I did, after a fashion. I said Philip Beydon had hired me to investigate his daughter's death, that he'd had a change of heart in midstream and had fired me. The way I put it, and without going into all the details, I said there were circumstances which made it pretty tough for me to back out now, if not impossible. I said I thought she might be able to help me out.

If she knew about me already, she didn't show it. Later on, she said she hadn't seen him since before Karen died, which I believed, but for the moment her only comment was: "Yes, he's given to changes of heart."

She invited me in.

"I never met Karen Beydon," she said, putting me in a two-seater couch under the front windows and sitting across from me. "Of course I heard about her. What was she like?"

"I never met her either," I said. "From what I know though, a pretty screwed-up girl."

"Yes," she said thoughtfully, and then without much hemming and hawing she launched into her own side of the story.

Why me?

It could have been the old chestnut about telling perfect strangers what you can't tell your best friend. Or my blond curly locks. Or that she wanted to get some things off her chest and I was handy. Or else that I came for her help and she gave it to me straight out, without frills or tears or coyness.

Sure, and when the sun comes up in the morning they'll be giving away free lemon pies in the bakeries.

What she said shortly was:

"You're a Leo, aren't you?"

"That's right," I said. "How'd you know?"

"I can always tell."

A little later it came out that Twink Beydon was a Leo too.

(For the record, I'm Scorpio. Not that it matters. I'm

adaptable when it comes to horoscopes. The last time I looked up Scorpio in the ratings, it said we were cut out to be good farmers.)

In any case she used to work for him a long time ago, or actually for the ad agency which had the account for a company he controlled. This was back before Karen was born, when Twink would have been in his early thirties. At first, I gathered, it was a sometimes thing between them, he with his life and she with hers and no questions asked. And then not so sometimes. More like all the time and twice on Sundays. She'd quit her job, and he'd bought this same house for her and set her up in it, far from the hurlyburly of the cruel world etcetera etcetera, also the prying eyes of snoops and columnists, and there they were going to live happily ever after as soon as his divorce came through.

She seemed to hesitate just that one time, talking about his divorce.

"If it's about Karen's pedigree," I ventured, "I already know about that."

"Oh?" she said. "No, not that. But I'm surprised you knew. Who told you?"

"He did."

Shc seemed surprised at that too.

"Well," she said, "what do you know! It's always been such a dark secret, I wouldn't have thought . . . Do you suppose it means he's finally growing up?"

It came out without bitterness or sarcasm, and not wanting to disillusion her I asked:

"Was he going to divorce Nancy then?"

"Yes he was. Looking back, I couldn't say it was just because of me. It was a terrible blow to his ego, awful. Karen, I mean. But at the time, well, I loved him very dearly, I didn't think it mattered why he was getting divorced, only that he was. Then, when he changed his mind about it, I could have gotten out. For that matter, I could have gotten out since."

I thought of him standing in front of the portrait, lecturing me on men who are afraid to make mistakes.

"What made him change his mind?"

"He said Nancy wouldn't give him a divorce."

"Was that true?"

"I don't know. Maybe it was. But certainly he could have forced it under the circumstances, if he'd really wanted to."

"What kind of woman was Nancy Beydon?"

She smiled at me.

"I never met her," she said. Then: "It wasn't just her, though, it was the Diehl connection. Business. Or being married to the Diehls. He couldn't let go of it. He wouldn't let go of it."

She paused, reflecting.

"I don't know," she said. "That's what I've always told myself. For what? twenty years? it's been the party line. But it could have been that he loved her after all, in his way. Even without knowing it. He's a very complicated man, Twink Beydon. I gather you've found that out."

I didn't know whether I'd buy that or not. Sure, complicated and all that, but who isn't complicated once you get down to histories? Histories, for instance, like his Silver Star brother Alan. According to Margaret, Alan had gotten himself kicked out of college and Twink had made him join up—to "straighten himself out." Which, in a gruesome way, was exactly what had happened.

Anyway, if Margaret could have gotten out easily once, a couple of years later it would have been tougher, the reason being that in between she got pregnant. The father—there'd been no doubt whatsoever, she said with a smile—was Twink Beydon himself, and the boy John (was this Karen's "Twink Jr.?") turned out to be the same teenager I'd seen tooling the VW out of the driveway.

It must have been pretty nice for Twink to find out he could cut it after all. Better than nice, the way she told it. More like scoring the winning TD in the Rose Bowl he'd never played in.

Well, he was a Leo, wasn't he?

And all over again he'd been ready to chuck it for her, and his son. Only he hadn't, all over again. And there'd been other times when he hadn't, and hearing her describe them, hearing her tell the dream Twink Beydon was supposed to have dreamed but never got around to living, I saw him again in the sweatsuit with the towel around his neck laying the same shit on me. Only when he'd laid the same shit on me, he'd been talking about his legal wife and daughter.

"Don't misunderstand me," she said. "I've no complaints coming. We've been well supported. I'm not that pure either, I've had my good times without him," curling a finger through the side of her hair the way women do when they're thinking about it. "But then after Nancy died . . ."

Her voice trailed off, leaving me with Ellen Plager in my mind, and maybe all the other Ellen Plagers.

"But it didn't work out that way," she said levelly. "So I did the next best thing. Dumb romantic thing. Idiotic really, and not at all like me. But I changed my name."

She grinned at me. Maybe she could read my thoughts.

"I did it on the spur of the moment," she said. "I mean, it's *easy!* All you do is do it. I imagine if you wanted to change your name to Rockefeller, no one would stop you. Or Beydon certainly."

Then change it back, I told her in my mind.

"Friends of mine thought I was crazy," she said. "I guess I was. Am. Or getting back at him, but it wasn't that. It was just something I wanted to do, always had I guess, and so I did it. It pulled me out of a bad time. After all, from my point of view it was the truth, do you see?"

And weirdly enough, I did. Later on I might think her vanity must have come unglued along the way, and not only her vanity, because no number in her right mind is going to carry her torch that high. But at the time . . . well, if I'd stuck around her much longer, she might have had me believing in decency and love and God-knows-what-other of our time-honored values.

As it was, she offered me a drink, which I turned down.

"What about your son?" I asked her. It struck me he wouldn't have taken so kindly to her changing the family label, or to be being a bastard for that matter, or to having his old man hanging around all those . . .

She shook her head.

"No," she said. "Johnny's not that kind of kid. It's all right with him. He's got his problems, but he wouldn't have had anything to do with Karen, if that's what's on your mind."

I asked her if she knew anything about a letter Nancy might have written Karen, or if Karen had left a will. No, she said, she was afraid she didn't.

"Just one other thing. Apparently Karen knew about you. Do you have any idea how?"

"No, I don't particularly," she said, "but she did know. In fact she called me once—not that long ago either, a few months, as much as six maybe. I never told Twink. She wanted to meet me. She said a lot of other things that . . . well, that weren't very complimentary. I said I didn't think it would be a very good idea. I tried to explain, but she hung up on me finally. And that was that. I think now I should have done something about it, but of course you think a lot of things like that after the fact."

As for me, as I got up I was thinking: a nice woman, even if she was a damn fool it was a shame, etcetera etcetera. And that it had turned out a nice day after all, the sun was also shining nicely, and one nice thought led to another.

But I happened to glance out the front windows in between Nice Thoughts 2 and 3, and what I saw brought trouble back on the run. The Mustang had company and so did we, plenty of it. Some four or five cars which hadn't been there before were parked in the street around the house. The black Firebird was one, the gunmetal Ford another, and in a third I thought I saw my old and silent friend Gomez, who I hadn't run into since before his brother passed away.

14

"How'd you know it was my birthday?" I said to her.

"Your birthday?"

She started.

"But . . . I'm sorry, I thought you said you were . . ."

Then she saw them too.

"Who's that?" she said.

I wonder if she really didn't know, not that it made a damn.

"Well," I said, "unless somebody else on your street's throwing a party, I'd say they'd come for mine."

I counted noses—five that I could see—and decided I didn't like the odds. I glanced around the house, looking for the trapdoor to the tunnel which would take me out to some place safe. I didn't see any.

"Is there another way out of here?" I asked for the hell of it.

"Sure, there's the back door. But . . ."

She laughed, a little nervously.

"You don't really think they'd do anything like that?" she said. "Out here? In broad daylight?"

"I not only think so, I'd be willing to give you points."

"But who *are* they?"

I explained it, as succinctly as I could. At first she didn't believe it, that he'd do a thing like that. She said I was crazy, I must have made it all up in my head. I said that with all due respect whether she believed it or not or I was crazy was beside the point.

We stared at each other. She hesitated, and I headed for the door.

"No, wait," she decided.

She held out her arm.

"You're not going anywhere," she said firmly. "Sit down again and don't move. You wait there for me."

I sat down again. She left me. Quite some time went by, plenty of time for me to blow kisses out the window and think about my future. I figured she was trying to call him and having the same luck I'd once had back before George S. Curie III "relieved me of my duties." I thought of going outside and trying to parley, and I tried to picture what would happen if I waited for them to make the first move, and I came up with the same ugly scenario both ways.

But then suddenly I heard her voice talking, arguing, angry. It wasn't a short conversation either, but I didn't get up to eavesdrop.

Finally she came back and sat down next to me. She didn't say a word, but her nostrils were working overtime.

We watched together, like a silent movie.

A little later, sure enough, we saw the little wimp in the black Firebird jump in his seat. He picked up a phone receiver and listened to it, his head cocked like a dog's. His lips never moved. Then he hung up, got out and went over to each of the other cars, one by one. I was right, it was Gomez in one, also the guy with the elephant nose. They took turns shaking their heads at each other. Then the little wimp got back in the Firebird, and the motors fired one after the other, and they drove out the way they'd come, in a row, leaving the Mustang in the lurch.

It was magic, nothing less.

"I never knew I had a fairy godmother," I said to her, or some dumb thing, but she was gazing out the window and I don't think she heard, or when I said goodby.

I let myself out.

Her magic held. The Mustang and I got home all by ourselves, without escort. The apartment didn't explode when I opened the door, and there weren't any clicks on the phone, and the biddy from the answering service had a message for me from one of my lady friends. But it wasn't Robin this time, or Karen, or any of the other Karens, or anyone you've heard of, though for the record her name was Solange and she works for Air France. On the impulse—the oldest one there is—I called Solange back. She said she'd like to visit me, her longlost friend Cage, if I wasn't busy. I said I wasn't, on the contrary, and that if she'd give me time to put in some provisions I'd come pick her up. "*Bon*," she said, "O.K.," but, with a little laugh, would I mind getting provisions for three? And then on second thought, why didn't I forget about the provisions now and come for them right away?

Her friend's name was one of those hyphenated jobs beginning with Marie. She was very outgoing, this hyphenated Marie, and so was Solange. So was I. In fact one way and another we never did get around to the provisions until Sunday morning when I cooked them a breakfast like they don't get back in France, and then I took them back to bed in the sun and listened to them complain about Sunday flights, first with me in the middle, then Solange, then Marie, and they were still complaining when Solange finally took her hand off the throttle at the airport.

An interlude then. Beautiful. Or call it a hyphen.

Because when I got home, they'd already started filling in what came after the dash.

It was my Firebird wimp again with his cannon,

sitting on the edge of my white couch, and this time he'd brought Gomez along for company.

The aztec shut the door behind me.

I made a crack about having the locks changed, but nobody laughed.

"He's ready for you now," the little guy said. He stood up. "Let's go, Cage."

Well what do you know? I thought. All of a sudden the shoe was on the other foot, and pinching.

"Go where?" I said. "Now wait a minute, you guys. Hell, I just got home. You know how it is, can't you come back a little later?"

"Let's go," the little guy repeated, and Gomez encouraged me at the base of my spine.

"You'd better call him first," I said. I wasn't about to go anywhere with them, not till I had what I wanted, but at the same time I've never seen a fight I wouldn't talk my way out of if I could.

"We had enough of your funny business yesterday," he said, jerking his head in the general direction of the Valley. "Now he wants you brought in. That's what he said."

"Sure he said to bring me in. But number one, it's not me he wants, you know that. Number two, I've got it all right, you know that too, but number three, it's not here. Look for yourself. And number four is that if you take me in now without it, like he's never going to get it. Add it all up, sweetheart, it still spells Mother."

Around in there was when Gomez gave me a little tap. Just for nothing, I think, or maybe he was sensitive about his mother. I couldn't see it coming because he was standing behind me, but he sure didn't wind up from the floor either. All the same it sent the colored light zinging down my vertebrae and back up, and the bell rang in my head and I ended up on my knees.

The little guy cussed him out in Spanish and he backed off.

I shook my head to make sure everything was still there. I stood up, rubbing the back of my neck and watching Gomez out of the corner of my eye.

"Look," I said to the little guy, "I'm not trying to pull a fast one. All I want to do is talk to him first.

"Call him," I said.

We waltzed around with it a while, while Gomez waited to cut in. Finally I managed to convince him. I tried to guess the number from his dialing, but I got screwed up between a 7 and an 8 on the third digit and blew the rest. Anyway it wasn't Twink Beydon who answered, but you could tell when he came on by the way the little wimp popped to. Meanwhile Gomez was staring at me mournfully from across the room and scratching his nards.

". . . says he wants to do it his way," the little guy was saying. He didn't actually use "sir," but it was in his tone. "Yeah . . . O.K. . . . Right . . . ," and with a last "O.K.," he handed me the receiver.

"Cage? Are you there?"

Hey ole buddy, I answered in my mind, how're they hanging?

"That's right," I said.

"Look Cage, we're finished playing around with you. I want my property back, right now. Either that or you. It's up to you."

Just like the general addressing the troops all right: It's up to you, boys, either your nose in the shit or my boot up your ass.

"Like what are you going to do with me?" I said, staring back at Gomez. "Down in the squash court with your gorilla here and throw away the key? What would Margaret say?"

"That's my decision," he answered tersely. "You make yours."

"I've already made it," I said.

"I'm listening."

I had one card left to play, so I played it.

"You'll get your property, but I don't keep it lying around here. I guess you've already found that out. I've got to go get it first, and I'm not taking your Indians along. You'll have to call them off."

"That's a cheap trick, Cage. Why should I believe you?"

"That's your decision," I answered.

True to form, he made up his mind in a hurry.

"I'll give you till five o'clock, that's all."

It was a little after three.

"That'll make it a little tight . . . ," I began.

"Five o'clock, no more, no less."

"Maybe your brothers-in-law would be a little more liberal," I said.

He didn't bat an eyelash, at least over the phone.

"You bring it here," he said. "I'm at George Curie's office. You know the address. And let me tell you something, Cage—" he dropped his voice for emphasis "—if you're fucking with me now, it'll be the last time."

I didn't answer.

"Is that clear?"

"It's clear," I said.

"Then let me talk to Freeling."

Have a nice wait, Twink, I said in my mind, and turning to the room: "Hey, which one of you guys is Freeling?"

The little guy reached for the receiver, and I gave it to him. Gomez didn't so much as grin. His stare just kept getting longer and longer, like I was a *piñata* and somebody'd taken his baseball bat away.

"That's right," Freeling said, keeping his eyes on me, and "O.K." and "Yeah," and then he hung up.

"So you did it again, bud," he said to me, neither surprised nor disappointed. He put his cannon away. "So you got yourself another reprieve. But Mr. Beydon told me to make sure you got the message. It's your last one."

"Thanks, guys," I said, showing them the door. "I'll remember you both in my will."

When I came down about an hour later, they were still there, Freeling behind the wheel of the Firebird and Gomez standing next to it. It must have been one powerful itch, because the aztec was shooting pocket pool again, but they didn't follow me when I drove out of the garage, and later when I played a little hide-and-seek on the freeways just to make sure, I didn't spot them or any of the others.

I took Twink Beydon at his word. It was, like I say, my last card, my big play for the brass ring. Even before I left the house I must've had a hunch I wouldn't be sleeping there again for a couple of nights, or forty. I figured a suitcase would be too obvious, so I packed a toothbrush in my inside jacket pocket, and I even got out my dusty old musket from the dresser and loaded her up, though later I stuck her in the glove compartment for safety's sake. And then I took a shower, a shave, said so long to myself in the bathroom mirror, and got dressed for church.

15

I think I called it "one of our less savory neighborhoods." That must be the euphemism of the year. Oh they've put the new Convention Center down that way and called it urban renewal, but it'll take a hell of a lot more than one measly Convention Center to bring civilization, Doris Day style, back to those parts.

South San Pedro? It's warehouses and markets, and a string of Chink restaurants that look like Seoul, Korea, the morning after the earthquake. They've got rats as big as cats down there—yeah, rats, honest to God, Doris—and the freeways up above in the sky belong to another world. You go out a little further and it's spadesville, solid, where they peddle the dope in six-packs and the law drives around in bulletproof vests shooting at anything that moves. And after that, it's Watts. At night down there you can feel Crime roaming the streets, with bloodshot eyes and a shiv up his sleeve and a sweet hip way of talking that makes your blood run cold, and even on a Sunday afternoon in May you keep your windows rolled up and your doors locked.

A nice place to raise the family.

Five o'clock came and went and so did six. All this is for you, Twink baby, I said in my mind, but the dusty laugh which came back was my own. The bridges were burned all right, and I had an image of Gomez swimming the moat, tugging a pack of crocodiles behind him on leashes.

The address I wanted belonged to a warehouse which looked like it hadn't been used since they switched over to round wheels. It was locked up tight. The street, like all the surrounding streets, was deserted, and the windows, such as they were, were either boarded over or black-painted. There weren't any signs except for some graffiti in chalk, the most printable of which was "Louis sucks," and even allowing for his proverbial humility, it was tough to imagine Mr. Christ picking it out as the place to make a comeback.

I drove around it, stopped, and drove around it some more. Once I drove downtown, just to make sure downtown was still there. I had a couple of Chivas in the Biltmore bar, which was about as deadly as you'd expect on a Sunday afternoon, and then I went back. Still nothing. I thought of calling George S. Curie III's office to find out if a guy named Cage had showed up yet, then thought better of it. I thought maybe Christ had changed his mind, which was another thought I didn't like to think about. Finally I said the hell with it, pulled my stomach together and drove around to one of the Chink joints on San Pedro.

About six of the natives were at the counter, three on either side, watching the tong wars on a TV set which Chiang must have taken with him when he blew the mainland. The three on my side were eating, and I figured if they could take it so could I. I slid into a booth, tucked my pigtail under a bib and dug into a bowl of seaweed soup, with a side of fortune cookies. Strange as it may sound, I even had seconds on the Moo Goo Gai Pan, and stranger still the whole mess stayed down.

It was dark when I went back again, and for a minute

I thought I'd taken the wrong street. Either that or I was late for church. There wasn't a parking space the length of the block, and they were big cars too, Buicks and Mercs, with a dash of foreign, what you'd expect maybe in a Baptist parking lot on Sunday morning, but off South San Pedro? I had to turn the corner and go almost to the next one before I found a slot for the Mustang, and then I walked back behind a squat little guy in a business suit and mustache who looked like he might have hustled clothes over on Westwood Boulevard.

I followed him to the warehouse door, which had only a single light behind it in a kind of entryway, then another door, and blocking it was a tall blond kid, Andy Ford style but bigger, and barefooted, and he was wearing one of those long rough brown robes of the model St. Francis introduced way back when. The coat-and-suit merchant in front of me had his wallet out, and I saw a fifty-dollar bill go from his hand to the kid's to a money box on top of a wood table, and there wasn't any change coming back. Then the kid stood by to let him through and it was my turn.

I could hear the music through the door and some other people coming in behind me.

"You wouldn't by any chance take a credit card?" I said.

"Sure will, brother," said the blond kid. "Anything you've got, BankAmericard, Master Charge . . ."

I guess I was too surprised to do anything but fish mine out of my wallet and sign the chit when he'd run it through his machine. Things sure had changed since we used to pass the collection plate back home.

My contribution was also for fifty dollars.

"I hope it's worth it," I said to the blond kid.

"There aren't too many who go away disappointed,

Brother Cage," he said to me, handing me back my card and turning to the customers behind me.

I went through the door and into a well-lit vestibule with white partitioned walls. The music was coming from beyond the walls, an organ and a choir, or maybe the audience singing, and from what I could see, it may not have been St. Peter's in Rome but it wasn't any old warehouse either. A light show was playing on the ceiling, a row of spots focused on the altar and the stained glass behind it, but where the congregation knelt was pitch dark. I smelled a strong musky incense, more Indian than Catholic, and then a gust of perfume, and a voice was saying in my ear:

"This way, Brother. This way."

She was a big broad-shouldered number, almost as tall as I was, with short auburn hair that frothed about her face. She wore a white robe that gathered high under the neck with a clasp and a sash around her waist and ended at her bare feet. A white hood fell back off her head and her eyes had a gray-green cast and the white-toothed smile that came with the perfume made my knees wobble.

"I'm Sister Jan," she said gaily, taking me by the arm. "I'm your sister for this evening."

"But what about the service?" I said. "I . . ."

"We won't miss a thing, Brother," she said, flashing the smile again, "not a thing. I promise."

She led me down the vestibule into another room divided into stalls. I went along, thinking sex and God, God and sex, but not very hard. I glimpsed the coat-and-suit man being helped out of his suit by another sister, and not just his suit, and then Sister Jan did the same with me right down to my shoelaces. From somewhere she produced one of the hooded St. Francis jobs and draped it around me, tying the tie around my waist like a bathrobe.

The cloth was rough to the skin. I guess it was supposed to be.

"Why don't we just forget about the service, Sister Jan," I said vaguely, and she laughed, dipping her hair in my eyes so that the perfume half-blinded me, saying huskily, "Oh come on now, the others are waiting for us," or some such, the words no longer mattered very much, and back we went into the vestibule and around one end of the white partition, and she led me by the hand into church.

It was dark like I said, except for the colored lights on the ceiling and the spots on the altar, where a life-sized Christ was spreadeagled on a white cross. All I could make out following her down the aisle were the humpy masses of the faithful, but later when my eyes adjusted I saw brothers and sisters kneeling in couples on the floor, and all the brothers wore brown robes, the sisters white, and which were guests and which not I've no idea, except that some of the sisters looked twice as old as some of the brothers, and vice versa. There was sand scattered all over the floor, but it only hurt your knees a little while. The faithful were singing, and the incense so strong it blew down your pipes and out the other end, and the organ, which had to have been a tape amplified a thousand times, caromed off the lighted ceiling, the walls, and all but lifted your voice out of you.

"Sing along," Sister Jan whispered to me, squeezing my hand, "sing along, Brother." So I sang, and she never let go my hand while we knelt near the back. Others came in behind us, shadowy in their robes, kneeling and singing, until the music stopped with a gigantic organ chord rolling out of the L.A. hills, loud enough to bring down Jericho by itself, and another tall blond brother stood up in his Franciscan robe before the altar, extending his arms up and forward over the congregation, saying: "Would all you Sisters in Jesus please come forward now?"

It was Christian all right. It was also pagan, and aborigine, and turned inside out and unscrewed at the bellybutton. It was tactile and visual and processional. It was taste, sound and smell—a regular sensual catastrophe and all of it Jesus. The weirdest part—and a tribute to whatever mad freaked-out mentality had concocted it—was that if it was cockeyed at first, then it wasn't half so cockeyed only a little.

And then not at all.

It made perfect sense all right.

First the Sisters in Jesus went forward. Sister Jan went forward in a long shadowy swirl of white. She joined the line in front of the altar. Another brother stood beside the altar, a silver bowl in his hands. One by one the sisters knelt and kissed the Lord Jesus chastely. Then one by one the sisters took two of the wafers of Jesus from the silver bowl. Then Sister Jan came back to her brother with the two wafers of Jesus, and kneeling in the sand before him fed one to his tongue and the other to her own, and sealed their delivery with her lips. Then Sister Jan knelt in the sand beside Brother Cage, squeezing his hand, and together they bowed their heads to the prayer of Brother Philip, a prayer that made no sense at first but then began to make perfect sense, a prayer of thanksgiving to the Fairest Lord Jesus, hosannah, a prayer of union for the souls and bodies of the Brothers and Sisters of the Fairest Lord Jesus, hosannah, a prayer for the Fairest Lord Jesus to make His face shine upon their Adoration of His whole Body, hosannah, a prayer for Brother Pablo in his ministry this evening over the faithful community of the Fairest Lord Jesus, hosannah, a prayer for joy and singing, hosannah, a prayer for hope and love, hosannah, a prayer for understanding and community and the giving of each sister to her brother and each brother to his sister, hosannah, hosannah, amen.

All this, as I say, began to make perfect sense, and so it did for all the congregation to stand for Brother Pablo and to kneel again, and for Brother Pablo to be a little brother in the brown Franciscan robe with the light glancing off his specs like hailstones banging off the windowpanes, and for Brother Pablo to take his specs off while he preached and let his eyes shine out darkly over the congregation, preaching in a voice which wasn't loud or soft but so slowly you could watch the words coming out of his mouth in waves. Slow lazy word waves danced over the flower people, up one row and down the other until they got to Sister Jan and Brother Cage, in their ears and down into their bellies and making Brother Cage so light before they went back out the other ear all he had to do to fly was lift his arms, just like Brother Pablo lifted his arms over the heads of the flower people like wings. And the incense wafted through his wings and glided him into the air like a feather. And he circled like a kindly bird, waiting for the flower people to join him which they did, riding on his tail in a swarm of brown and white wings. And Sister Jan went with them up above the multicolored sky across the carpet of L.A. all the way to the sea, then curving on the curve of the hills, making the lazy rim of the great gray bowl in the sea of darkness, Santa Monica, Hollywood, Griffith Park, Elysian Park, dropping powder as they went, silver and gold, which scoured the sky and washed it clean and fell like snow on the good people of Los Angeles huddled in their homes where it never snows.

All this, as I say, began to make perfect sense. And it made perfect sense for Brother Cage not to fly, shivering in the brown robe and feeling his stomach start to twist and churn because he couldn't. And for them to come back down through the multicolored sky looking for him because they'd missed him. And to find him shaking like a leaf in a crosswind because he couldn't fly. And for the four-eyed Brother Pablo to say:

"Come on, Brother! All you have to do is fly!"

And for Brother Cage's teeth to chatter, and for him to answer:

"I can't fly."

And for the four-eyed Brother Pablo to say:

"We can't wait much longer, Brother. It's now or never."

And for Brother Cage to answer in a whining voice that wasn't even his own:

"I can't. I don't know how," feeling the empty yawning gulfing pace where his stomach used to be.

"Sister Jan will show you how."

And for Brother Cage to answer:

"Sister Jan isn't here," and looking up, to see Sister Jan smiling down at him behind Brother Pablo, a long way off but so close he could reach out and touch her. And looking up, to see Brother Pablo's Chink and Drummer eyes staring down at him, bulging out of their sockets like twin brown oranges, and the fingers drumming patiently, impatiently. And hearing the drumming fingers like paint dripping on the roof of his head, for Brother Cage to squint his eyes and start to cry, hot like a baby, the tears oozing out like Mel Tormé singing "Blues in the Night," and the cold empty place once they'd gone. Until a few thousand years later Sister Jan brushed the wet from his face and took his whole ear into her mouth, whispering:

"Fly, Brother. You can fly now. Stand up and *fly!*"

So Brother Cage stood up unsteadily with the flower people, Sister Jan with him, and flew! Yes *flew!* Brother Cage linked hands with the flower people and the silver-wheeled chariot came riding down the rainbow and Brother Pablo flogged the horses and the song surging up out of the lost caves inside him because it went back as far as he went back to the First Presbyterian Church of Yakima in the State of Washington:

"Fairest Lord Jesus . . .

"Ruler of all nations . . ."

And it made perfect sense that Brother Cage should fly. It was normal even. Normal too when the hymn to the Fairest Lord was over and the call came out for the brothers and sisters to come forward separately, that he should join the long line waiting before the Altar. And what could have been more normal than that, when his turn came and he kissed the Fairest Lord spreadeagled on the cross, a great booming ribsocking belly laugh should come busting out into the smithereened air, a laughter that was his because written across the wheels in his head were SEX and GOD and across the ass-end of the chariot SEX and GOD, a laughter that was long gone in any case in the roar of incense and stained glass and the flood of altar lights? And what more normal than that, when Brother Philip passed around the silver bowl, offering the wafers to each, each to feed onto the tongue of his brother or sister, Brother Cage should have taken one and fed it to her, and she to him? And what if the sister who fed him his wasn't Sister Jan, not her at all but Sister Robin Fletcher in her place? And what if it wasn't Sister Jan but Sister Robin Fletcher who took his hand then and led him out of church into the cloistered corridor where the stalls gave off on either side? And if the stall to which she took him, closing the door behind them, wasn't Sister Jan's but Sister Robin Fletcher's?

"Fair are the meadows . . .

"Fairer still the woodlands . . ."

Yes it made perfect sense, all of it, there in Jesusland.

16

There were moments back in Sister Robin's stall when Brother Cage seemed to know he was me and I him, but they didn't last very long. Mostly he was Ben-Hur or Don Juan or Romeo Montague, with a little of Twink Beydon thrown in, and for him to give me breathing space he had to do the Atlas bit, pushing them all through his neck and out his skull and balancing them on top. He wasn't much good at it. Sister Robin didn't help at all and neither did the Heavenly Host, or whatever it was we'd swallowed. Sooner or later Brother Cage'd let go the whole load and it was every man for himself, like a couple of thousand tons of elevator with the pulleys cut loose, whummmmp, while he went up about five thousand feet or so, taking his flying lessons.

It was dark in the stall. All it was probably was the old shipping room partitioned off into cubicles, each with a cot, a sink and a threadbare piece of rug on the floor, and a poster of Him on the wall and under it a mini-altar with a candle burning on top because they'd blown their electricity money on the church. But for Brother Cage it was the real McCoy, like what he'd always known went on inside the nunneries, and nothing would keep him from getting down on his damn fool knees and praying his head off while Sister Robin worked him from behind like a milkmaid under a cow.

Sister Robin looked like hell, even in the dark. Her

face had gone all the way through flour to something else and her eyes were a couple of holes somebody'd dug in the dirt and forgot to fill in. But it didn't matter to Brother Cage. Sister Jan, Sister Robin, Sister Eleanor Roosevelt, all the same and all the Queen of Sheba.

Like early in the game I managed to get a word in sideways:

"I'm here to talk, Robin," I said, and Robin Fletcher started to giggle, and she said, "Sure sweet baby, that's all we're gonna do," meanwhile pulling Brother Cage by the short hairs at the back of his neck, and in he went to a pair of dugs which weren't much for a girl her build, at least at a glance because then the elevator started down again and the damn fool went out of sight.

It was hard to tell which of them was more stoned. Sister Robin came on like she'd been on something for a year of weeks, whereas Brother Cage had only been hit twice; but on the other hand Sister Robin had the candy-bar habit and Brother Cage didn't. Maybe when it comes to stoned there's a plateau everybody gets to sooner or later where it's all brothers and sisters and love and Jesus and happy time, and people come on like a pack of screaming hyenas that have been penned up ever since the good fathers lowered the boom on sex.

Anyway, no sooner would Brother Cage come down than I'd have to start climbing up again inside, up through all the shit that had come unglued inside him. Twink Beydon was there, and the Drummer, and Karen, and all the Karens, and Margaret Beydon because all of a sudden she reminded him of Mrs. Hotchkiss in the third grade, and George S. Curie III, and Andy Ford because he reminded him of himself, and Nancy Diehl Beydon and her brothers and Jesus and Sister Jan and Brother Pablo flogging the horses and all the people who'd done him in and all he'd done in, all the grabbers and the people who got it taken away. And some of them had slanty eyes and others round, some were people he'd forgotten about, some gave him the hot sweats and others cold, and his emotions went down and up in waves all the way from Panicsville to Disneyland like a rollercoaster where the dips never get any smaller. Every so often I'd get up within shouting distance of him and yell my bloody head off for him to forget about brothers and sisters and love and Jesus and happy time and remember what he was there for: like money, scratch, bread, loot, lucre, dough and Cage's Old-Age Retirement Plan and Slush Fund, and sometimes he'd hear long enough to ask the dollar-sign questions. But then Sister Robin would start to prime his pump again, and Brother Cage beat up on her till she screamed bloody murder, which didn't make any difference because from the acoustics back there you'd have thought it was the San Diego Zoo on Saturday nights when they let the baboons loose on the giraffes, and it was all I could do to hold onto the answers inside, such as they were, and keep 'em from flushing on out with about ten million live spermatozoa.

Somebody ought to have brought a camera.

Come to think of it, maybe somebody had. At least it figured to be part of the racket.

Because a racket it was, although the way Sister Robin told it you had to splice all the pieces up and glue 'em back together again to make them fit. It hadn't started out that way. It had started out a bunch of nice young redblooded California acidheads looking for something stronger to turn them on and coming up with the Great Man Himself. Karen Beydon, you could say, had opened up the southern branch, which included Robin and Andy Ford and a few others, and later on they'd merged under the main tent up in L.A. Along the way somebody had come up with the idea of turning it into a paying proposition, that being Brother Pablo mostly though Andy Ford had had a hand in it, and in the best American style: that is by raising capital (from Karen among others) and hard work and plowing the profits back in and paying the law to look the other way. To judge from the turnout and the collection plate, business was one hell of a lot better than in the regular Sunday A.M. Christ parlors, and according to Robin they were making improvements all the time.

By this time Sister Karen had long since dropped out of the organization. Brother Andy had gone after her, except that Brother Andy had taken most of the sacramental wine with him and opened up shop for himself. Which made Brother Andy about ten steps lower on the Jesus scale than the Devil himself, and if he ever showed his nose around the Society again there wouldn't be any resurrection. Sister Robin had been supposed to go with him but somehow she hadn't made it. That set Sister Robin off on one long Andy Ford jag, and her Andy Ford jag set her off on a what's-going-to-happen-to-Sister-Robin jag, because if she went outside in the cold Andy Ford'd cut her heart out, and if Andy Ford didn't cut her heart out Brother Pablo would, and all this because what she'd given them she'd taken away, and Brother Cage had to go up and get her, or down, and the screen went blank again for a while.

And what had she given them that she'd taken away?

Nancy's letter. Nancy Beydon's letter to her daughter Karen.

O.K. And when had Nancy Beydon written this letter?

Before she died.

Had Karen gotten it then?

No, Karen hadn't gotten it till later.

And how had Karen gotten it?

The lawyer had given it to her.

What lawyer? George S. Curie III?

George S. Curie III. On her twentieth birthday. Happy birthday, Karen.

Oh. And what had Karen done about it?

Karen hadn't done anything about it, except go see the lawyer.

Oh. And how had Sister Robin come by it?

Sister Robin had taken it with her after Karen jumped.

And she'd given it to Brother Pablo after that?

Yes. It was kind of a rule, Jesus' rule, like with the early Christians. Either she'd given him a piece of it or the whole thing, enough for him to start shaking down Twink Beydon in the name of Christ our Lord. Only then he couldn't deliver, because she'd taken it back.

But why had she taken it back?

On account of Andy Ford.

On account of Andy Ford?

That's right. She and Andy Ford were going to make it together. She and Andy Ford had always been going to make it together way back from the beginning when she'd read it in the stars. She had it bad for Andy Ford, she'd always had it bad for Andy Ford even if they didn't have two sticks of incense to rub together. Only now they did so why didn't he come back, Andy? she'd make it nice for him again, it'd be grand, the same old song, except this time she was going down on Brother Cage while she was singing it, right down on his star-spangled banana, and sure enough the sparks started flying in his skull, the roof of his skull lit up like the sky above Yakima, Washington, on the Fourth of July, ker-BOOm, ker-BOOm, her-BOOm, and the goddam screen went white again.

O.K., so Andy Ford'd had the bright idea of using it to shake down the Diehls, right?

Right. Only Andy Ford couldn't deliver either, because then she'd taken it back.

But why had she taken it back?

Because she was scared. Because she was scared of Brother Pablo. No, not because of Brother Pablo, because of Brother Cage. She liked Brother Cage, oh she really liked him, she always had, she'd dug him right at the beginning, she'd been scared Brother Cage was going to get his head handed to him if she didn't take it back, yes that was it, it was so long ago she could hardly remember, she'd wanted Brother Cage to ball her right then, right at the beginning when he came along . . .

So she'd taken it back all because of Brother Cage?

Or almost all. Because she was scared of Brother Andy too, scared he didn't love her enough, or maybe he did, maybe she could make him, but there was only one way she could be . . .

So she took it back?

Right. She went and took it.

So where did she go?

She went to Number 63, Blue Pacific Villas.

To Number 63, Blue Pacific Villas. But somebody was there ahead of her, right?

That's right. Tito Lopez was there ahead of her.

Tito Lopez was there ahead of her. So what did she do to Tito Lopez?

She balled Tito Lopez.

She balled Tito Lopez? But wasn't Tito Lopez dead yet?

No, Tito Lopez wasn't dead yet. Tito Lopez had what she wanted. Tito Lopez didn't want to give it to her.

So then what happened? Did Robin kill Tito Lopez?

Robin killed Tito Lopez? Maybe so. Maybe Robin killed Tito Lopez. Right through the eyeball—POW!

So then what happened?

Then she took what was hers and she took off.

Oh.

So then Brother Cage asked the first half of the

$64,000 question. So what was in the twelve handwritten pages of Nancy's letter to Karen that made it so valuable to Pablo and Andy and Twink Beydon and Andrew and Boyd and Bryce Diehl Jr.?

And Robin Fletcher *told* him, after her fashion!

And Brother Cage hardly heard!

Because Brother Cage, the Franciscan, was down on his knees where he liked to be, making like a mole snuffling in the roots, and Sister Robin was riding on his head, hanging onto his ear with one hand and waving the other in the air like a cowboy making the Last Roundup, her hair over her eyes like a haystack, screaming her freaked-out lungs off about Karen Beydon's parentage and all the whores of Twink Twike Tweek Twuck and how she wanted Brother Cage, Jesus God she wanted him RIGHT NOW, and Nancy spelling it all out for Karen how she could fuck him if she really wanted to, really fuck him once and for all like she Nancy had never had the guts to, and C'mon darlin', take it all, take it now, it's all yours, Oh Jesus I'm so stoned, it was all in the will, the letter and the will, whose will? Nancy Beydon's will? what will? Oh the will! and the giggle and the cackle and the godawful laugh that tore the dead out of their graves all the way back to the Pharaohs rotting in their tombs . . .

"*Nancy's* will? *Nancy's* will? No goddam it, fuck me, Cage, Oh God, FUCK ME, CAGE! Grandpa's will! *Grandpa Diehl's will!*"

I drove up Brother Cage then. I drove inside his back and up his neck. I drove clean into the roof of his skull like a pile driver blasting through the shit of him and into the solid rock. His head went flying in a million pieces and he looked down inside and saw me hanging onto the cobwebs and I shouted at him: Ride her, you son of a bitch, Ride her! And he said: Where you been, old buddy? like I'd just come out of the grave. *Ride her!*

I blasted at him, and he shouted back: Now you're talkin', now you're talkin' ole buddy, climb aboard!, seeing that I was him and he was me and that there was no we any more, just old Lonesome Cage, the one and only, riding down the trail of broken hearts. And so I heisted old Robin Fletcher up in the air like a sack of meal, she hanging on for dear life—"Fuck me, Cage, sweet Jesus God honey if you don't fuck me I'll die"—and down on the rusty nun's cot with her, flat on her back where she wanted to be, where she always wanted to be, so she said, with her legs hanging in the stirrups high up above her head and her hands reaching for it, wanting it like they always do, the old love muscle, the horn of the bull, and I let her have a little of it, just enough to keep her reaching, saying:

"Where is it, Robin? Where's Nancy's letter?"

She started to wail, she started to moan, she started to hiccup all at once. She started to die right there and then just to show me she knew how, with the hair flying across her face like tumbleweed blowing down the highway.

"I'll tell you, Cage. Jesus God, I hid it. Only it's long gone. It's so lo-o-ong gone, Jesus God, I'll never go back there again, nobody ever will. Andy, my God, when're you comin' home Andy . . ."

I let her have a little more, and her legs pretzeled tight around my back, fighting for it with her thighs, and I fought the bubble back inside, the great big snow bubble oozing out my brain and sliding down the spine column, saying:

"Where's Nancy's letter, Robin? Let's have it!"

She screamed, she wailed, she bit, she tore, she belted my back with her fists. Oh she died all right, a thousand times or so in a second. And she told me. She told me, the lying bitch, she told me, and I believed her, believed her enough to let the bubble go south down the pike, and her legs went wide, wider than wide and rocking, and she opened up like a clam when the water starts to boil, and she came in a blast of blasts, farting all the way, and she shouted:

"Look out, Cage! Jesus God Almighty!"

I ducked, but not far enough. Another stronger blast belted me into the wall. The bed went over, the altar somersaulted, the whole room rocked and tilted. It was the Brethren, about a dozen of them or fifty, busting all at once, busting the door clean off its hinges, busting me, busting Robin, and then I was on my hands and knees fighting for my life in the dark, slipping and sliding like the whole earth had turned to mud, and I heard Robin screaming and laughing in the corner, that bad wild unearthly sound.

If they'd come in three or four they'd have had me, but as it was I left them fighting themselves. I tunneled through, and under. A foot kicked me in the head. Somebody had a hammer lock on my neck for a while. I let fly and felt the soft crunch of nards, heard the shriek, and the grip fell apart. A tearing sound behind me where somebody's sleeve had torn loose. It was my own. I came up and through them like a drowning man flailing for the light. I hit the corridor on one wheel, slipped, skidded and cornered. On my feet and running, while behind me all hell broke loose. It was the Zoo on Saturday night all right, and Bedlam when they unloosed the bats, and all the stoned of California screaming on an overdose.

The church was dark, empty. The light show had gone out, and the multicolored sky was just a crummy warehouse ceiling. The only light was the spot on the Fairest Lord. If it hadn't been for him and the lying bitch behind me, I could have gone right out the front door like any old night watchman on a coffee break.

Sorry ole buddy, I told him in my mind.

I didn't stop running. I hit him like a pulling guard leading the sweep, and his head flew off in one direction, his body skittered on the sand in the other. Papier-mâché Jesus. The altar top came loose in my hands, lock and all. I reached inside for the goodie and came up with the collection box and a stack of handbills. I reached again. Nothing. I stuck my head in and poked around.

Sister Robin had pulled another fast one. Even stoned and scared and shivering and wild and coming like a runaway train, Robin had pulled a fast one. Jesus Christ, Doris, what kind of monsters have they let loose on this earth?

I didn't have time to worry about it then. I didn't have time to worry about anything. The lights went on and the Avenging Angel stormed into the desecrated temple, leading his monks. They came out from every rock, pore and crevice, St. Francis' gang, except that these days the Avenging Angel wears glasses and he packs a gun instead of a sword.

They stopped a second when they saw me.

I threw the cash box at Brother Pablo, just for nothing.

The gun went off in my ear. The bullet went in that ear and out the other and splintered the colored glass behind me. Lucky thing. Not that my head was empty, but that it showed me the way.

I went out behind it. The gun splattered behind me and the colored glass smashed and showered just like it does in all your dreams and all your trips, only this time it was real.

17

I landed on my knees, fell forward, rolled and took off. I ran like Roger Bannister going for the four-minute mile, and when I'd run the four-minute mile I did another, and when I stopped long enough to feel myself hurting all over I ran again. It's easy enough now to say I was running for my life, but on the spot it was something a lot worse. It was the monster risen up behind me some twenty stories tall, and laughing that bad wild shrieking laugh. It was the whole town gone amok, freeways torn loose by the roots, buildings powdering like houses of clay, the pavement of the goddam streets going zizzle-zazzle under my feet. Call it the wedding of King Kong and Godzilla, with the Beast from Twenty Thousand Fathoms carrying the flowers, and when the laughing started it twisted my mind like a cruller to realize it wasn't the Beast laughing at all, or even Robin Fletcher, but the sirens of the law carousing through the night.

And longer still to understand who it was who'd called the law down. On the spot it was only Twink Twike Tweek Twuck, who'd gotten tired of waiting out at George Curie's joint and had blown the bugle, which meant every cop and deputy and California Highway Patrol and National Guard from here to Seattle, all of them hunting for something as inconspicuous as a white man running around spadesville in a one-armed monk's robe and nothing else, and bleeding like a stuck pig.

It was only the next day that I finally tumbled. Because if not Twink, then who?

The papers told me. The papers made a barbecue out of it with all the trimmings. Like: "We all know and deplore the depraved activities some of our children have become involved in, even to the point of travestying our most revered institutions, but what does it mean when older, respectable citizens start to join them?" Back on Page 3 were the names, chapter and verse, including some of the respectable citizens and a picture of a Paul Meier, the "ringleader," who was none other than Brother Pablo, and all the others I knew about. All, that is, except one. The last time I'd seen her, or heard her, she'd been screaming her head off and stoned out of her crazy mind, but stoned or sober, I guess it made no difference to Robin Fletcher when the crunch was on. Maybe the brothers had doublecrossed her, maybe not, but she'd had enough cool to slip out and call down the law, and then . . . ?

Well then, I guess you could say, Robin Fletcher had busted out.

And as for me?

I was beat, done in, run to ground. I mean, you figure it out. A stoned and one-armed monk in spadesville in the middle of the night, without so much as a dime to make a phone call. What was I supposed to do, start ringing doorbells?

I ended up in a drycleaning store in some godforsaken shopping center. I must have busted in the door. No alarm went off that I remember. I guess they can't afford them down there. At that, who'd have come even if an alarm went off, the law? I mean, it's not exactly Fashion Square down there. Spadesville, friend.

I hunkered down in some clothes in a bin under the

racks, and that's where I crashed. Up until then the adrenalin must have neutralized the acid working my system, enough at least to keep me moving when I had to move, but now the acid, or whatever it was they'd sugared the wafers with, got even with a vengeance. My face was cut in a hundred places, and each one started to hurt like all the mortifications the monks ever invented. Every sound, every creak, got decibeled up to rats galloping across the roof, and horses galloping across the rats. I did the hot and cold bit, and to top it off my chest started itching like a son of a bitch, and I scratched it till the hairs caught fire and I tore the goddam sackcloth off, and then the bell rang and my teeth broke out of the starting gate, doing sixty by the time they hit the backstretch.

I also started seeing things. I remember there was a heap sitting out in the parking lot, the only one I could see from where I was. I was staring at the heap, and the more I stared, the more I was pretty sure the heap was staring back. Then it started toward me, crawling like a dismembered bug or a tank with one of its treads missing, but crawling, and it crawled right up to the dry-cleaner's window till its nose was pressed up against it, making a mist. I jammed myself down into the bin, my heart going off like the gong at the end of Dragnet, and the next time I looked the heap was back where it'd been and a gang of bloodshot moonriders were stripping it of everything that wasn't welded down, like hubcaps, tires, wheels, headlights and the roof rack up on top. Maybe I dreamt the part, and when they started carrying TV sets out of the emporium next door, and I didn't have to pray to whoever was listening that they didn't decide to help themselves to some clean clothes while they were at it. But when I saw the heap again it looked so godawful mutilated that it was the last thing I saw for a while.

How long?

You tell me. It was still dark when I finally climbed out of the bin and called her. Even that took some doing. I figured there had to be a phone somewhere, like next to the cash register, but I couldn't find the cash register. When I did, the holes in the dial got as big as the Hollywood Bowl, and when I dialed and she answered I got the giggles for no reason I remember, that kind of hysteria that doesn't have much to do with comedy. She all but hung up on me. Then when I'd explained and she wanted to know where I was, I spent a couple of days or so on my hands and knees till I found the drycleaner's order pad.

I'll leave her name out of it, also her phone number. I called her because she was the only person I could think of who wouldn't ask a million and one embarrassing questions. It was the old flame bit, very old. Since then she'd turned pro and was doing fine for herself, and a couple of times back during Cage's personal recession she'd thrown some business my way. Who she had to kick out of bed or what kind of a crimp I put in her schedule I've no idea, but a while later when the headlights swung into the shopping center, they were real, and they were hers, and I crawled out and into her back seat and that was the last thing I knew until we started picking bits of glass out of my face with a tweezers the next day.

I still hadn't come out of it all the way. I drank enough bouillon to keep the meat extract people in business till Lent, but I couldn't handle the orange juice. It was the waves again, only finally the crests got further and further apart and in the end the sea went flat like a bathtub, and it stayed flat. We watched the Society of the Fairest Lord Show on TV, including all the reruns. In the afternoon she went out and bought the papers, also some clothes for me, which she put on the bill. She was itchy for me to leave, I could see, but when I told her I couldn't go home because some friends of mine were using my apartment, she bought it without too much squawk, and she was making some phone calls when I fell asleep again.

I woke up a little after midnight.

I was brainstorming like Albert Einstein thinking up relativity. The windmills were spinning, all the windmills, and Robin Fletcher was telling me again how she'd hid the letter and how long gone it was, lo-o-o-o-ong gone, where she could never go again etcetera etcetera, not ever, while the title of a book I'd read once bumped into it like a car going against the traffic.

I ran it through my head a couple of more times and listened to it, the parts that weren't smudged out. Then I let the book title in where I could see it. And then . . . I had it! Where I'd find the letter, and Robin Fletcher too! Of course! Elementary, Dr. Watson!

Dumbass.

Before I could think it through the rest of the way, I tripped over my own congratulations. In other words I made a mistake—the more so because no sooner done that I compounded it—but the way it worked out, my last one.

I got long distance information on the phone. There were only two Fletchers in the book, and I hit mine the first try. It was Robin's old man who answered, and I probably woke him up because his voice had that suspicious who-the-hell's-calling-at-this-hour fuzz to it. But it didn't matter. Nosireebob, Arthur Fletcher, it didn't matter. It was like one of those puzzles where you slide the little balls around under the glass, trying to slip them into the holes, and I had them all in but one, and after I got through talking to Arthur Fletcher, I was all set to take off right there and then.

Only I let my hostess talk me out of it.

I'd've sworn I'd sworn off sex for the duration, along with God, but what the hell, just for Auld Lang Syne . . .

I told her to put that on the bill too, along with the cash she lent me. Which she did, as it turned out. Which made it a little bit like love.

In the morning she drove me back downtown to Jesusland. Man's Best Friend was still there on the street, looking pissed off but none the worse for wear. Amazing, but not a thing was missing, not even my keys in the ashtray, and the only addition was a day-old parking ticket under the lefthand wiper.

18

Normally it's a three, three and a half hour drive. We made it in a little under two and a half, the Mustang and me, even allowing for a pileup coming over the pass where a truck had run into another truck and the CHPs were still scraping the pieces off the freeway. I hadn't been up that way in years. On the run north I usually take the coast road because it's prettier, and it's a hell of a long way to go just to buy a bushel of grapes. But it was still there, the San Joaquin, as flat as the palm of your hand and a lot richer, also hotter, the towns looking about what they'd always looked like and no sign of that weird morning fog they get up there.

The night before, I'd told Mr. Fletcher I was Robin's doctor. I told him she'd disappeared and that I was worried about her condition and that under no circumstances was he to let her leave till I got there. I told him I was on my way.

He was an ineffectual old geezer, closer to seventy than anything else. If he'd believed me over the phone, he sure didn't in broad daylight, on his front porch, though I suppose it didn't help that my face looked like the last barber who'd worked on it had had St. Vitus' Dance.

"Can't you people leave her alone?" he said in a whine. "You're the one who said he was a doctor, aren't you? I could tell. Hasn't she been through enough already this . . ."

But then a voice I recognized broke in behind him: "It's O.K., Daddy. I know who it is."

She looked old. She was wearing one of those shapeless gingham housedresses and you couldn't see the little-girl-in-the-sandbox no matter how you tried. Come to think of it, I guess we all looked pretty old, standing there. Arthur Fletcher looked old enough to be her grandfather, which he probably was in years. Robin looked old enough to be his daughter, which she was. And me? Well, I could've been the guy who'd brought her kicking and screaming into the world, which I wasn't.

She sent her old man back to his whittling and took me into what passed for the living room. Maybe she was embarrassed about it, but she needn't have been. Like I'd been there before myself: the upholstered wicker furniture, the curtains that couldn't take another washing, the footstool with its guts hanging out the bottom. All that was missing were the *Reader's Digests* and the *Geographics*. Maybe in Tulare County they kept them up in the attic.

"You can't go home again," I said, "is that it, Robin?"

She grinned at me halfway and sat down. I did too, feeling all of a sudden not only old but tired, used, and not so bad about it either because for the first time in longer than I could remember there was no rush, no hurry. The last little ball had slid into the hole.

Sure it had.

She said she felt the same way as me, wasted, she said. She said she'd give me what I wanted, she was tired of running, she couldn't make it any more. But first she wanted to talk a little. She said she felt like talking if I didn't mind listening. Would I mind listening a little while, she asked me?

I guess I was feeling pretty big-hearted. I mean, everybody's supposed to get his last wish, etc.

I told her I wouldn't mind listening.

She started in about Karen's mother. She was a cold frigid bitch, she said, I'd understand once I'd read the letter. Not that you could blame her, given what she was married to. It was awful, she said, the way people screwed themselves up getting married. She didn't think she ever would. She didn't think she'd ever get married, she meant. Look at her own parents, she said. I'd seen her father, what was left of him. What was left of her mother was in a sort of half rest home, half asylum, up on the other side of Fresno. She told me all about her mother and father. Sometimes, she said, she wondered how much of her mother she'd inherited, but when that got to her too much, all she had to do was take a look at the rest of the people running around on the loose. She guessed there wasn't a funny farm built that was big enough to hold them all. Sometimes she thought that was all the world was: a great big funny farm.

I gave her an I for Insight. Then, to bring her back to a topic of greater mutual interest, I asked her what was in Bryce Diehl's will.

She told me, mostly. When she was done, I couldn't keep a soft whistle from coming out. It wasn't just the money then, it was the power that went with it. And all of it Karen's.

Maybe Grandpa Diehl had outgrabbed them all at that.

"How'd you find out about it?" I asked her.

"Karie told me."

"After George Curie told her?"

"That's right."

I began to see why Twink Beydon had gotten so exercised. Only what had taken him so long? "I haven't seen as much of her as I should have," he'd said once, where if I'd been in his shoes I'd've been down on my knees in front of her washing the linoleum before she took a step.

"And then Karie died," I said.

"Yeah. Poor Karie."

"Which changed all the equations around. Did you push her, Robin?"

It seemed like I'd asked that question a thousand times before, but I got the same answer.

"No, like I said. She was busting out. I really think that's what she was doing: busting out. I guess I could've stopped her, but . . ."

She bit at a knuckle to show she was feeling bad.

"Poor Karie," she said.

"And then you took off with the family jewels."

"That's right."

"And they were off and running at Santa Anita."

She giggled a little.

"Tell me something," I said, "why'd you send me the journal? Was it just so I could read her poems? And why'd you call me up?"

"I liked you, Cage. I needed you, I really did."

"Yeah, and you also thought I was still working for him, didn't you? That maybe I could be your way in? And what about when I showed up the other night, is that still what you had in mind?"

"Like I say," she answered, "I liked you."

She smiled at me, a sideways smile. So help me, she even ran her fingers down the hair alongside her cheek.

"Sure you liked me. Like your brothers liked me. Everybody likes me."

"They had me set up," she said. "Both of us. Pablo

knew all about you. They kept me zonked the whole week in case you showed up. They thought I'd tell you where it was."

"And you knew that's what they hoped you'd do, didn't you?"

"Well . . ."

"And you figured out a pretty good way to get rid of most of the competition, honh, all in one little lie? With a phone call to the law to put the frosting on the cake?"

Just then while I was talking I may have had a little flicker inside, no more.

"Tell me something, Robin, were you really stoned?"

"Like there's no way of faking that, man, is there?" she said. "No way."

Amazing. And to think of me, while she was setting us all up, down and under in the drycleaner's clothes bin. A question of experience, I guess.

"It's too bad," I said magnanimously. "If you hadn't diddled me around so much, maybe I could have figured out a way to cut you in."

"You didn't seem the type, Cage."

"The type?"

"To cut people in on anything."

"I'm not," I said, "any more than you're the type who writes poetry."

That seemed to piss her off. Of all things. Her face went tight, and without any warning she started hollering at me:

"What makes you think *you're* such a hot shit? Look at you! You've got it all wired, haven't you? Right! That's how you get your rocks off, honh? Oh you've got it wired all right, sure you have! You're real clever, and you've outthought everybody, Mr. Bigshot Cage! There's not a man in the world you can't outthink, is there? Or a woman who's not gonna cream her jeans just at the sight of you? Oh right, right! Oh right . . ."

The flicker again, stronger. I'd been nice enough long enough.

I stood up.

"O.K. Robin, you've said your piece. Now let's have Nancy's letter."

She didn't budge. Instead she began to laugh, that cackle sound that curled my ears. The flicker became a twitch and all of a sudden all of the little balls shook loose in the glass puzzle and started to roll around again.

"*Let's have Nancy's letter! Let's have Nancy's letter!* Listen to him now, Mr. Bigshot Cage! What makes you think I'd give it to you if I had it? You'd have to cut my heart out first, you bastard! You're late, *Mr.* Cage! You're too *late!* And all while we've been sitting here shootin' the breeze! You've fucked up, Mr. Smartass Cage, and now I don't think you're ever gonna get it!"

Her cackle went up one wall, across the ceiling, and down the other. Then her knee came up, ready, and it stopped me cold.

I reached for my musket.

The laughter died down. In its place came tears, and I guess they were real enough though with Robin Fletcher I wouldn't take bets. They ran down her cheeks and wetted up her hair like hay left out in the rain.

"Go ahead, Cage!" she shouted. "Do you think I give a damn? He's gone now, long gone, and I'll never catch him, and neither will *you!*

"*Sure* I gave it to him!" she howled, seeing the look on my face. "After you called what did you think I was gonna do? Sit here and *wait* for you? He's ten feet taller'n you, Cage! Than you'll ever be! *Sure* I called him! He drove all night, which is more than you ever did! And he *beat* you, Cage! *We* beat you, me 'n' Andy!

We beat you by an hour and now it's more, every second. So what you gonna do, Cage, *shoot* me? Sure, go ahead Cage, shoot me!"

"You dumb cunt!" I shouted back at her. "D'you think you'll ever see him again now? D'you think he's coming back for *you?*"

She didn't have to answer. She just peered out at me with that cockeyed lop-ended teary grin on her face.

"So long, sweet baby," she said hoarsely. "Have a nice day."

She was asking for it so, was that the only reason I didn't give it to her? I glanced down at the musket. It looked absurd, stuck there in my hand. I put it away.

Then I lit out, leaving her singing the last chorus of the Andy Ford blues. I punched the Mustang into action and turned her loose. By the time we hit the freeway she was wide open, and any cop that wanted to stop us would have had to call the Air National Guard for help. It was then or bust, and if I was going to end up with spaghetti for dinner, I'd just as leave have eaten it in hell as Santa Monica.

At that I'd hate to have had to bet on my chances. He could have gone south or north. Heads you win, tails I lose.

I picked south.

She'd said he had an hour or more head start, and that made it tough odds even for Breedlove.

But it must have been less. Either that or he'd stopped for coffee, or to count his money before he had it.

I guess we're all entitled to one mistake.

I caught him even before he'd made the top of the pass. The cream-colored van all right, black curtains and all. And out in the fourth lane doing like eighty uphill, which is about twice what any van is entitled to do, it says in *Road & Track*. But no match in any case for the Mustang on a dry strip.

He saw me.

He started to zig and zag from lane to lane like he expected me to try and pass him, over in the third and back into the fourth, back into the third and over in the second, all the way into the first and back out again. He was good at it too.

I sat on his tail and admired his style.

Hell, what was I supposed to do on four lanes of freeway, pass him? And then what? Try to run him off into the island or the shoulder, take your choice? After all, it'd only have been paying him back for what he'd done to me once.

But no sir. That wasn't *my* style. I wanted what he had, not him, and I wanted it in one piece, clean and legible, with no charring around the edges. So I sat on his ass, right up close to give him something to think about, and we went over the pass that way, zigging and zagging and braking and accelerating— Oh he was a cute one, he was—and started down the other side, the L.A. side, past the lodges and the motels they've got up there, and then I guess he started thinking overtime. Or stopped altogether.

In other words he made a second mistake, just like I had and just as dumb, and you'd have to say it was his last one too.

19

Some years back on that particular road, they had quite a headache with trucks running out of brake on the grades and causing general havoc among the downhill populace, not to say themselves. I mean, you figure that sea level is some four to five thousand feet down from the top of the pass, and you put Joe Truck on the downgrade loaded up to the earlobes with lettuce and take his brakes away, and it doesn't even take high school physics to imagine the salad he's going to make by the time he comes to a dead halt. It used to be great reading at breakfast along with the comics.

Finally the highway engineers went back to the drawing board, and they came up with a series of emergency runoffs spaced out all the way down. Escape hatches, you could say, or a kind of highway ejection seat. So nowadays when you get that uneasy weightless feeling where there's nothing under the brake pedal but floor and the gear shift comes loose in your hand and the little voice starts shouting, "Bombardier to Pilot, Bombardier to Pilot, we've been hit, sir, is it O.K. to bail out?" You're supposed to answer, "Leave everything to me, boys, hang on to yer cocks" and make for the nearest runoff, and if you kill yourself that way, well, at least it spares a lot of civilians.

Like I say, Andy Ford made a mistake. Meaning that

he tried to pull a Cage, and not a bad idea at that, except that it had occurred to me too.

A few miles down from the crest he zagged over into the second lane, and he stayed there. I zagged over behind him, and when he didn't zig back for the next half-mile, his mind was all spread out before me in big boldface type with plenty of white space between the thoughts.

He waited till the last second to try it. Then he blew across the truck lane doing eighty and he hit the runoff square on the money.

I went right behind him. I won't say it didn't give me a turn. The Mustang fought it. She sucked in her sides and wallowed and screeched her ass end and generally fried rubber all over Interstate 5. But when I opened my eyes again, all I saw was California mountain vista and ZNV 218 square in the middle of the picture.

It must have panicked him. I mean, by that time I was supposed to be halfway down and no place to turn around till I got to Hollywood and Vine. It had thrown me too when the Firebird showed up in my rearview that night on the Diehl Ranch. But then I'd had my unknown friend at 22 Acacia Drive, whereas the only friend Andy Ford had left in the world was me.

He made the first curve all right, and then he ran out of macadam. The surface turned to dirt, and a cloud of dust showered up and over my windshield. Even so I saw him go. There was a second hook sharper than the first, and halfway around it the van did its two-wheel number, a shadowy teetery dance with death. Then it must have hit something which kicked it over the rest of the way. It squealed on its side like a dragged steer. Then it flipped on its head and some rocks tore its scalp open in a spray of sparks. And over again . . . and again, like in slow motion, clunk . . . and clunk . . .

Then another clunk.

Then nothing.

The Mustang all but went after him. I threw out the anchor. The wheels skidded, spun dirt, held.

It was all over in a couple of seconds, but when I got out, the nerves in my legs were shaking like jumping beans. I ran down the slope, expecting the explosion that never came. The van was scrunched against a bed of rocks, its four wheels up in the air like legs. I climbed up its flank and got the door open on the passenger side. Everything had shook loose. The eggs had scrambled, the butter had curdled and the medicine chests had spilled out their guts in a junkie's paradise.

As for Andy Ford, I guess he wasn't ten feet taller than me any more. He was mashed against what used to be the window of the driver's door. If he wasn't dead already, his head didn't look any too secure, lolling that way off his neck.

It would be nice to say I hung around there, thinking up epitaphs. I didn't. I found what I was looking for laying on the seat next to him, like he'd left it there for me. I took it. It was in a Number 10 envelope addressed to Miss Robin Fletcher at the address he and I had already visited that morning. I checked it out, enough to see the Dear Karen and the first paragraph, and then before you could say "Only the good die young" I was back behind the wheel of the Mustang, driving down the runoff a little further till I found a spot to turn around, then back out, off the dirt and onto the macadam, and off the macadam and on my way.

The law made a big thing of it. I suppose you can't blame them. The *Times* ran it in their another-pusher-meets-his-fiery-end section, but whether that "fiery end" was the rewrite man's imagination or the van had gone up in smoke after I left or the law lit a match to it for reasons of their own, I've no idea. There was even an interview with my there-is-no-local-drug-scene sheriff who said they'd been shadowing Ford for weeks, trying to find Mr. Big, but no connection to Karen or Robin or me, or anyone you know.

End of obit.

I drove down through the earthquake country around Sylmar, taking it slow and easy. Where the freeway splits in two, I got off. Time was on my side for a change. Before my next stop, like the lady said, I wanted everything wired, all the circuits plugged in, so that when I threw the switch it came up Bell Fruit Gum, once twice three times, and not a wheelbarrow made big enough to cart away the silver.

I put the Mustang in a carwash and walked across to a W. T. Grant's. I borrowed their copying machine—at 10¢ a sheet it came to $2.40—and I ate an omelet at their counter with a side of German fries and a couple of cups of what they called coffee. Then I picked up the Mustang and drove around till I found a U.S. Post Office. I bought a stamped envelope, an extra stamp because of the weight, folded in Nancy Beydon's original, addressed it, licked it, sealed it, and dropped it in the slot. A little more complicated than Robin Fletcher's method, and though I'm not about to divulge any trade secrets, if you picture a baseball diamond with Cage on third, Cage on second and Cage on first, you'll have the skeleton of it. If Cage in the middle ever muffs the doubleplay ball at a pre-arranged time and place, well then, the old scoreboard blows up and the game is over. Call it the Tinker-to-Evers-to-Chance system, Karen's notebooks were already in it, and I guess at that it's pretty foolproof.

And then over a couple of scotches in an aztec saloon in San Fernando, I made the acquaintance of Nancy Diehl Beydon, posthumously.

Twelve pages' worth of Happy Birthday Karen, on both sides, and written in the kind of perfect slanting script you don't expect to see any more, except maybe among the finishing school set. She hadn't been in any hurry. There weren't any smudges or scratchouts or wavery lines, and for a while I was thinking Karen's brand of hysteria had to have come from some other hereditary line, which wouldn't have been Twink either. And maybe so. But looking at it another way, you could say that Karen's notebooks were what Nancy's letter would have been if the right upbringing, plus twenty-some-odd years of marriage to Twink, hadn't squeezed the juice out of the lemon, leaving nothing but an even monotone, with the i's after e's except after c's.

She wrote like she painted, meaning flat, unemotional, and in a way that was worse. By the time I was done, I'd have settled for twink twike tweek twuck. Because with Karen, well, you could always say she was freaked out, stoned, or that it was fantasy, or that it was just the younger generation dumping on the older; but Nancy reminded you of those people you see fishing every so often who drop the fish back in the water once they've caught him, with the hook still in his mouth, just for the pleasure of catching him again.

The fish, of course, was Twink.

Or maybe it was the other way around, take your choice.

To make a long story short:

It had been a nightmare, she said. When he'd found out she was pregnant, he'd wanted her to have an abortion. She'd refused. She'd wanted Karen more than anything in the world, she said. Instead, according to her, she'd offered him a divorce. He'd turned her down. Karen's real father hadn't been anything more than a passing fancy to her. She'd never seen him again. Twink had always let it be known he'd paid him off, but she had good reason to believe it was more than that. He was dead, she said. She knew how he'd died. She'd never had the courage to try to prove it, but she told Karen how if Karen felt otherwise.

She had stayed with Twink for form's sake, and for Karen's. She accepted Karen's condemnation of her for having done so. Looking back, she believed she even shared it. She asked Karen to try to understand, however. Yes, she'd had grounds for a divorce since (here she went into the story of the tramp Twink had taken up with, one Margaret Tanner, their bastard included, and what that had meant to her), but she'd never been able to bring herself to initiate it. That was her weakness, her fear of scandal perhaps. Instead she'd built her life on another basis. She'd found another way to pay him back.

The one thing he wanted, she said, she'd been able to deny him. That was control of the company. Left to themselves, she thought, her brothers (Karen's uncles) would have long since capitulated to him. He'd wanted to make a public offering of the company's stock, that was his technique, and she'd thwarted him. She alone. More than once he'd tried to convince her: how much money it would mean to them all, how it made sense from a purely business point of view and so on. The last time—a scene she described with as much relish as I guess she could allow herself—he had even proposed in exchange the divorce she'd once offered him.

"It was my great pleasure to refuse him," she wrote to Karen.

And why had she finally decided to unburden herself of the truth? Why this letter, after all the years? It was because she was dying, she said. She knew she was, and perhaps it was just as well. She even had her own medical theory to go along with it: that the deception of her own life had made her susceptible to cancer.

And now, you could say, she was passing the truth on to Karen, along with the rest.

"When I was twenty-one," she wrote, "I did something against my father's advice. It was a big step, and I was very young. How often I've wished I could have told him he was right.

"But now, Karen dear," she wrote, "you're going to have a choice to make, also at twenty-one. What I suggest you do, once you've read and digested this letter, is to go to George Curie and ask him to show you your grandfather's will. The rest will be up to you, and you will have three years to think about it and make up your mind. It is in order to help you that I'm sending you this rather ghastly confession of the truth.

"May God bless you and keep you, darling."

Read cold, I suppose, and with the prose misted up a little, it might have had you reaching for your handkerchief.

You maybe. Not me.

Happy Birthday, Karen.

A discrepancy in that last paragraph interested me, but I filed it away. It wasn't the only one by a long-shot. Maybe you'd have to take Twink's version, and Margaret's, and Nancy's, not to leave out Karen's, and scramble them all together to get the family portrait in focus.

Even then . . .

But what got to me more was how little effect it seemed to have had on the Karen of the notebooks. I mean, you imagine getting a birthday card like that from your old lady. Well, you could say Karen was strung out already, also that it would have taken a mental retard to grow up in a household like that and not put a few things together. But it was more like Nancy had been talking to her all her life, that the letter only confirmed what she already knew in her bones. Like Twink, the murderer. Like a name for Twink's whore. Like that abortion detail, which gave her phony letter to Twink an extra twist of the knife. The more I thought of it, the more I thought: like mother like daughter.

Sure she'd've made up her mind already.

And then she'd jumped.

If she'd jumped.

I'd been playing with my loose change on the bar top. I picked the coins up again and dropped them and pushed them around in the wet till I had them all lined up in ranks like bright young troopers standing Reveille. They were singing out "*Here*, sergeant!" and listening to them gave me that warm, feet-up-by-the-fire feeling. I ordered another scotch by way of a salute. Not that what it added up to was necessarily the whole bona fide cross-my-heart-and-hope-to-die truth, but it would do. Oh it would do. They were all there, present and accounted for, all the bright young troopers. The only one missing was the C.O., and I had his spot zeroed in nicely in the crosshairs.

It was dusk when I came south over Sepulveda Pass. The rush hour was long since over and all the Valley breadwinners back home and finished dinner and settled down for the Tuesday Night Movie. I wave them goodby. Out toward Santa Monica the sky was a deep deep purple. I headed east from the freeway, past UCLA, the gates of Bel Air and into Beverly Hills, and by the time I pulled off Sunset onto Doheny, the deep purple had lost its nerve.

What did I say? That I'd have settled for twink twike tweek twuck?

Then make a wish. Because that's exactly what I got.

20

I'm going to give it to you the way you want it first. Otherwise it'd spoil the poetry.

Poetry? Well, I don't know what else you'd call it, unless you want to figure Twink Beydon and his shyster had been sitting there holding hands for the past forty-eight hours, waiting for Lonesome Cage to ride in with the Pony Express. As for me, I'd expected maybe a cleanup woman or two, or if I was lucky that receptionist number boning up on her law, or unlucky, Miss Sensible Shoes polishing her lorgnette. Or most probably, nothing at all but an alarm system to worry about.

But that's why I hustle for a living instead of writing poetry. I mean, you put the scene together: a soft night falling onto Beverly Hills, Lonesome Cage riding up on his trusty Mustang, clippety-clop, clippety-clop, Lonesome Cage tethering his Mustang to the hitching post, giving the joint the once-around, walking around to the shyster's private office where the lights were on, looking around the corner of the window and spotting in the library . . . who? two chambermaids polishing up the spittoons?

Not in this ballad, friend.

So Lonesome Cage tested the front door, locked, and drew his trusty six-shooter. He blasted a hole through the lock big enough to drive a team of mules through.

He kicked in the door and climbed into the library, spurs clanking.

The cattle-rustler looked up from the table where he was shuffling the pasteboards. The shyster looked up too. The cheroot fell out of the shyster's mouth.

"We been waitin' on ya, Lonesome," said the cattle-rustler. "How're they hangin'? You want I should deal ya in?"

"Ain't got time, Big Twink," said Lonesome Cage. "Brung somethin' you been lookin' for."

Lonesome Cage unbuttoned his shirt pocket, pulled out the papers, dropped them on the table.

"Read," said Lonesome Cage.

The shyster reached for the papers. Lonesome Cage shot a hole through the shyster's palm, about as round as a silver dollar, about as clean.

"Read," said Lonesome Cage.

Big Twink read. The nerves commenced to jump in his jaws.

"I fold, Lonesome," said Big Twink when he'd finished. "The game's over. You win. It's all yourn."

Big Twink pushed the chips and the paper money across the table. He pushed the gold and the silver across the table. Then he looked up at Lonesome Cage, his brows in a question mark.

Lonesome Cage said nothing.

"You name it, Lonesome," said Big Twink. He got up, knocking his chair over.

Big Twink went over to the wall safe, his back to Lonesome Cage. He fiddled with the wall safe dial.

"You name it, Lonesome," said Big Twink over his shoulder.

Big Twink had the wall safe open.

"Ain't money," said Lonesome Cage. "It's your ass."

Big Twink commenced to laugh. His whole body shook with the laughing.

"My ass!" said Big Twink, laughing. "My . . ."

"Ain't me who wants it neither," said Lonesome Cage. "It's Karen."

Big Twink stopped laughing. He froze by the wall safe and his eyes rolled in their sockets. He reached inside the wall safe and came out with the Gatling Gun. Even before he turned around the gun was going off in his hands. It spit lead all around the library. It tore the chandelier out by the roots and sent it crashing to the floor.

Then the Gatling Gun jumped out of Big Twink's hands, and it quieted.

Lonesome Cage had put a hole about the size of a dime between Big Twink's eyes, up where the nose ran out of sight.

"Karen . . ." Big Twink said.

Them was his last words. He went down like the big wood, out in the forest.

Lonesome Cage put up his six-shooter. He rolled Big Twink over with the toe of his boot. He picked the papers up out of the mess on the table and turned to the shyster.

"Got a light?" said Lonesome Cage.

"Sure Lonesome," said the shyster. "Jesus . . ." handing him a match with his good hand.

Lonesome Cage held the papers up in one hand and lit them with the other. He held them up while they burned. He watched them burn till the flame went out between his thumb and his forefinger.

"Thanks," said Lonesome Cage.

The shyster was shaking like a leaf in the big wind.

Then Lonesome Cage stepped over Big Twink's body, and he went out the way he'd come in.

He untethered the Mustang and climbed into the saddle.

Then Lonesome Cage rode west down the trail of broken hearts, and the sound of the lonely bugle followed him into the night, blowing "The Ballad of Lonesome Cage."

21

Only it didn't happen that way.

I mean, Lonesome Cage has a nice ring to it, and if you put it on my tombstone I won't mind at all, but I didn't even go in the front door.

I parked around the corner and walked the rest of the way. At night in Beverly Hills that's evidence of burglary—a man on foot without a dog or a number—but if Freeling, Gomez, etcetera were still out beating the cactus for me, I wasn't taking any chances.

Like I said, I'd made my last mistake.

I softshoed around the house and that's when I saw them in the library, through the window. Twink Beydon was staring right at me, in his shirt sleeves. His tie knot was pulled halfway down his shirt, the collar button open, and he was gesturing with an open palm while he spoke.

It gave me quite a turn. I still don't know what the hell the two of them were doing there at that hour, except that they must've had plenty to talk about once I didn't show up for tea on Sunday. Or were they waiting for someone else?

Poetry. Sheer poetry.

But the fact is: I never liked poetry. Also I'd no intention of tête-à-têting with Twink, not until I'd read Bryce Diehl's last will and testament all the way down to the nickels and dimes.

But on the other hand . . .

The front door had that strong silent look. It was also locked, and one of those wrought-iron lantern deals was hanging over it, all watts go. I could have lonesomed the light, but suppose the lock held? Or suppose it let loose the Baskervilles?

I circled back to the back. I mucked around in some shrubbery till I found another door. It must've been for the help once, but these days it only got used once a year when they delivered the booze for the Christmas party.

It was locked too, but there are locks and locks.

No alarm, no Baskervilles, nothing.

I found myself in some kind of pantry, maybe. I waited there in the dark, making a rough mental map of the premises. Then I did my No Man's Land special: one foot up and bring it down, but slow, lest you step on a foreign object, like a booby trap. I found a door that way, opened it, and entered a sort of storeroom filled with office furniture. Either the light got better then, or my eyes did. I opened another door and came out into the reception hall.

There wasn't anybody there to take my name.

I opened another door, quietly, and the light got a lot better. I went down three stairs and crossed a room on tiptoe, then stopped in the shadows.

That door to the library was open too. Three more steps up and there was Twink Beydon, his back to me, his ass about on a level with my nose. I could hear him talking. He happened to be talking about some son of a bitch I'd never heard of, name of Cage.

Poetry.

George S. Curie III was writing something down on a pad.

Twink twike tweek twuck, I said to no one in particular. Then, girding my loins—You only go around once in life, buddy boy—up the stairs I went.

George S. Curie III saw me coming. His eyebrows yo-yoed up and stayed there. He opened his mouth, but nothing came out. Maybe he was watching the redcoats coming back from Bunker Hill with their ass in a sling.

Big Twink saw George S. Curie III see me. He half-turned in his chair, started to get up, but no more. I gave him a gomez on the back of the head, low down on the right side. He sat back down. I bent over, checked him out, and then I gave him another one on the left side to balance things, and he slumped in his chair like a bum sleeping in a railroad station.

George S. Curie III was on his feet too, like some-body'd poured hot tea right in his lap. He was looking every whichway. Where're the redcoats? he was saying, where's the law? where's my secretary?

I pointed the musket at him, and he stared at me.

"You look like hell, Cage," he said. "My God, what happened to you? We ought to call a doctor, we . . ."

"Calm down, George," I told him. I waved the barrel of the musket at him. "You can call the doctor later. Meanwhile we've got some business to attend to, you and I. We don't want any interruptions. I don't use these things much, but I guess you know I wouldn't mind if I had to. So if anyone calls, or the Fuller Brush man rings the bell, you tell 'em you're busy and to call back later, right?"

He glanced at Twink, then back at me. I don't suppose he liked the sight of blood.

He nodded.

I took the copy of Nancy's letter out of my pocket. He knew what it was all right. I saw the little greedy gleam flash through his eyes, then disappear when he realized it wasn't the real thing.

"Sorry to disappoint you, George," I said, "but what did you expect? The original? It's in a safe place. Very safe. I'll want you to tell Twink all about that when he wakes up, some other things too. But first I think we ought to have a look at Bryce Diehl's will."

"Bryce Diehl's will?"

He did the eyebrow bit again for me. He said he didn't think he could do that, and he started to give me a lot of bullshit about confidentiality.

I cut him short.

I told him I could always get it the long way round, which he knew. Didn't he know that? Yes, he guessed he knew that. Only it would take time, I told him, and I had better things to do. And if he didn't go get it, I'd lay him out next to his client and go find it myself. And I'd make a hell of a mess while I was finding it, he knew that too, didn't he? And who could tell what else I'd find along the way?

He caved in. I suppose the George S. Curie IIIs always do.

As it happened, we didn't have to go anywhere to find it. It was sitting right there in a bunch of papers on the table beside his chair. So much for confidentiality. I also took a gander at the pad of yellow legal paper he'd been writing on when I came in. A shot in the dark maybe, but when I flipped the pages they smelled an awful lot like the draft of a stock prospectus to me.

"You were being a little bit previous there," I said, grinning at him, "weren't you George?"

He didn't answer.

I sat him back down, pulled up a chair and started to read. I read it all too, though I didn't have to. It always interests me to see how the rich operate when they realize they can't take it with them, and you could say that Bryce Diehl had left little to chance or the tax people. There were codicils within codicils, trust funds within trust funds, bequests, foundations, you name it. Most of the fortune went to his four children, but even that was so hedged and hemmed and footnoted in that I had to get George to explain some of it. He did too. I guess he was proud of his handiwork, or George C. Curie II's. All in all it was quite an education, and I'll have to keep it in mind when I get around to remembering my grandchildren.

But then I got down to the meat of it, what all the fussing and fuming was about, what had given Nancy Beydon the hammer lock on Twink, and Karen after her, and gotten everybody so exercised once Karen kicked off.

Before he died, Bryce Diehl had formed InterDiehl Holding, the big daddy of all the family enterprises. He left it to his four children, and he left them full control of it: Bryce Jr., Nancy, Andrew and Boyd. Left them control? Hell, he dotted the i's, crossed the t's, and damn near chained them to the fencepost. What it meant, once you got through all the legal shrubbery, was that no change in the status of the corporate setup could be made for ten years after Bryce Diehl's death, and after that only with the full and unanimous consent of the four. Any one of them could block it, and if and when one or more of them died, the power passed on to his or her children. And if they were minors? Then, according to George S. Curie III, the setup was frozen until they reached their majority. And if the children died before they reached their majority? Then, according to George S. Curie III, their rights, powers and obligations passed on to their next of kin.

Oh.

So that Bryce Diehl had taken care of the son-in-law he'd never met, even from the grave. Had taken care of him as best he could, if not till Judgment Day at least into the generation beyond him. I could imagine Twink's face when he first found out about it, like reaching for the prime ribs and finding out his wife's old man had just wiped the platter clean.

There was a question in my mind about whether it was legal or not. I mean, if you can't take it with you, how far ahead can you tie it up? George S. Curie III admitted it was a good question. It had never been answered because only the courts could decide it, and as a practical matter . . . Well, George S. Curie III intimated, once you started dealing with the more delicate rackets, such as city-building, dependent as they were on the good will of politicians, planning commissions and other fixers, it didn't pay to air the family linen. Better the end piece of beef than none at all, right, Twink babe?

So Twink had had to bide his time. He'd brought the Diehl brothers around, but he couldn't budge Nancy. Oh he'd given it the old college try, but somebody had taken the megaphone away from his cheerleader. And when Nancy died, he'd had the moratorium to sweat out till Karen reached twenty-one. But when Karen died ahead of time, why then it was open season, first come first served—unless, that is, someone could throw some doubt onto Twink Beydon's next-of-kinship.

"There's no question about that," George S. Curie III said.

"How do you know, George? You didn't represent him when Karen was born, did you?"

"I checked it for him once."

"For him, George? Like when? Say, a couple of weeks ago?"

He didn't answer. For a while there he'd been mighty helpful, friendly almost, but now he was back on the defensive, all closed up in his George S. Curie III Savile Row lining.

"The Diehls didn't think so, George."

"It's solid enough," he said. "It would stand up in court."

"Sure, and maybe take five years to stand up by the time they got done with him. And meanwhile what's to keep the Diehls from changing their vote, like tomorrow morning?"

"He can take care of the Diehls," George S. Curie III said.

I didn't know how and I didn't ask—one seamy story was as much as I could handle—but probably he could have at that, unless they had what I had. After all, George S. Curie III suggested, the Diehls were interested in the money too.

"On his terms?" I asked.

"If need be," he said.

A standoff then, between brothers and brother-in-law. But if Brother Cage could be persuaded to hand over the letter to Brother Twink . . . ?

By this time I'd about had it with brotherhoods in general.

"Tell me something, George," I said. "When did he realize she hated his guts?"

"Who, Nancy? Why . . ."

"Not Nancy, George. Karen."

"Karen? Why I'd no idea she . . ."

"C'mon, George. *You* told him, didn't you?"

"Me? How would I have known a thing like that?"

"You delivered the letter, George. Two years late, but you delivered it. And she came to see you. You showed her the will—this will—and I bet she told you right then what she was going to do to him, didn't she?"

He was staring down at his hands, that cookie-jar look.

"Tell me something else. What took you so long to deliver it? It was supposed to go to her on her *eighteenth* birthday, not her twentieth. But you took a peek, didn't you? And you decided to sit on it. For two years you sat on it. Why didn't you sit on it forever?"

I answered it for him.

"Let me guess," I said. "When did the Diehls fire you? Let me see, it was right around then, wasn't it? Sure it was, eh? And it panicked you, you of all people, George. I'm surprised at you. You'd run out of Diehls, all of a sudden after all those years of a free ride you'd run out of Diehls, and it made you shit quarters. Because as far as the Diehl Corporation was concerned, it left you with Twink for a client, who wasn't even on the board, and besides we all know how changeable Twink is, he'd as soon can you as look at you. So sooner than be left out in the cold altogether, you did a dumb thing. Maybe Twink had done a dumb thing by neglecting her, but you did an even dumber one by trying to latch onto her. You sent her the letter. For her twentieth birthday instead—better late than never, eh?—and when she came to see you, I bet you even tried to persuade her to make it up with him. Didn't you? Only she didn't listen, did she. She wasn't the type to take advice. She probably told you to go fuck yourself, collectively and individually, if she didn't laugh in your face. And that panicked you even worse.

"You only had one place left to go," I said, "didn't you."

"When did you clue him in?" I said. "Was it before she died, or after? Something tells me it must've been before, George, what d'you say?"

He looked up at me, that sad-faced son of a worm. He wasn't sweating outside, not yet, but inside it must have been running down in rivulets.

"You know," he said to me, "you're a dirty man. A profoundly dirty man."

"Well like they say," I replied, "it takes one to know one."

Before I popped the next one, I measured him carefully. It was the big one, the last of the big ones, and I didn't want to miss a thing. Probably he knew it was coming, but sometimes even when the logic is written on the walls, you close your eyes.

I let him wait for it, and then I said sharply:

"Do you really think he killed her, George?"

It shook him all right. His heart jumped up into his cheeks and he had to swallow it back down. It took him three tries. Still, I'd have sworn the idea wasn't new to him. On the contrary, it was that somebody else shared it.

After all, it stood to reason. Why else would he have hired me in the first place for a coverup job?

Only Twink Beydon had had another idea, hadn't he. Sure, Twink Beydon had called me down to Bay Isle, had done his father's guilt routine for me, had even let the great dark secret out of his bag. Knowing, hoping at any rate, that it would lead me to the missing evidence.

And why was that?

Because in between, Dr. Watson, a certain Brother Pablo had begun to sweat him about it.

I'll say this for George S. Curie III, whatever he knew or suspected, he fought it down to the end. Twink Beydon a murderer? Preposterous! A tough man, yes, even ruthless when he had to be, but to murder his own daughter? It was laughable. Besides, where were the witnesses? Could he have walked into Karen's dormitory in broad daylight and out again without being seen? Highly unlikely. Besides, the police had checked him out along with everyone else, hadn't they? Why he hadn't been within miles of the campus that day!

Like they'd checked out Robin Fletcher, I thought to myself.

"He didn't have to have done it himself," I said.

"There are plenty of people around who'd push someone out a window if the price was right."

"That's fantasy," he said. "Pure fantasy."

And so was all the rest of it: pure dirty-minded fantasy.

I let him run it down, just the way he might have in court. Then I asked him:

"What about her father, George? Was that fantasy too?"

"Her father?" he said with a start. "Who?"

"Oh c'mon George, you read it too, at least you read it in the letter. Karen's real daddy, you know? Nancy said Twink had him killed, she even told Karen how to prove it if she wanted to. Was that fantasy too?"

He shrugged.

"I couldn't say. I didn't . . ."

"I know," I interrupted, grinning at him. "You didn't represent him then."

You have to hand it to the shysters: if they don't represent you, they know from nothing.

"But you represented *her*, didn't you? Nancy? And was *she* a detective? Hardly, George. She said Twink had had him killed, but she wasn't there, was she? So where'd she find out about it? She had to go to someone for help, and who else but her attorney, good ole George S. Curie III? You ran it down for her, didn't you? Or more likely, you hired some stiff like me to do the dirty work for you."

He didn't answer, but his expression did. It was in between cookie-jar and Cheshire cat, and maybe it was my imagination that he blushed a little but I don't think so.

"And how *did* he die, George?" I went on. Because suddenly I *knew* it!

"Poor old daddy," I said. "I could dig that out too if I had to, but let me guess: Could it have been that he fell out of a window? Or was pushed? Like father, like daughter, now wouldn't that be one hell of a *coincidence?*"

Right on! his face told me. Right on the money! Bell Fruit Gum, Bell Fruit Gum, and Bell Fruit Gum!

And who was it said only the numbers've got intuition going for them?

But I didn't push it beyond that. There was no need to. Instead I laid out for him what I had for sure, all of it, plus enough of the Cage-to-Cage-to-Cage setup to convince him what would happen if anyone got any funny ideas about me and windows. I had the motive—in spades—and a modus operandi that would do for starters, and if there weren't any witnesses so far, who could tell what an ambitious district attorney might come up with once he started to dig?

It would never stand up in court, the indefatigable George S. Curie III told me when I was done. And I agreed with him. There was the admissibility of evidence for one thing. The long reach of Twink Beydon for another. I mean, everybody knows who goes to jail in this world and who doesn't, chances were it would have taken a lot more shut than open to put Twink behind bars. But like I told George, it didn't have to go that far. No, Your Honor, no sir. An indictment would do fine. Hell, the way I saw it even an investigation would have been enough to dry up his backers, because if there's one thing those goo-peddler types won't stand for, it's somebody else's stench bringing attention to their own. And then where would Twink Beydon have been? Like back taking potluck with the Diehls, if the Diehls would give him room at the trough. And from what I knew, he'd already waited too long, and maybe risked too much, to end up sucking hind tit.

I took a long hard gander at the man in question. We both did. I guess sleep must be the great equalizer for stiffs, like beauty parlors for the numbers, because he sure didn't look like a murderer, even by proxy. Not sprawled out that way, sighing like an overgrown baby, his chin tucked into his shoulder, the big beef cheeks spreading into jowls . . .

But then they say they never do.

And like I say, it didn't make much of a damn what *I* thought, and George S. Curie III must have come to the same conclusion about the indefatigable George S. Curie III, because finally he said:

"What's your price, Cage?"

I shook my head.

"It's not for sale," I told him.

He stared at me, surprised, so I told him about Cage's Old-Age Retirement and Pension Fund. I showed him how it worked from the inside out, just like the annuity hustlers do. Only this one was based on just one security—IDH, they'd probably call it on the Big Board—and a stock dividend went into it every year in addition to the original investment.

Sweet and simple. Very.

"But that's highway robbery!" he said, the greed flickering in and out of his eyes like a deaf-mute's code.

"You could call it that," I said. "Blackmail'll do too, hush money, I'm not particular."

I also wanted it in writing, with him for a witness. I gave him twenty-four hours to draw it up, get Twink to sign it and deliver it to me. In triplicate. A copy for Twink, a copy for me and a copy for George S. Curie III.

That part threw him worse than the deal itself. After all, the money wouldn't be coming out of his pocket, but putting anything in writing makes the shysters nervous, much less when they have to sign it themselves. Beyond that, he could see he was going to have to sell it to Twink when he woke up, and I think he was genuinely scared to. Not that he had much choice or that I had to spell it out for him, because my way he at least had a chance to keep his client and . . . no, George, there was no other way.

We had a last skirmish over the will, of all things. I wanted a copy of it for my archives, and he said that was *illegal!* I mean, he actually said it was illegal—privileged, confidential and so forth, you figure it out! In the end I had to march him in to his Xerox machine by the scruff of the neck, and he did the rest quietly enough. He ran each page through for me, and I made him certify that it was a fair copy and stamp it with his notary's stamp and sign on the dotted line.

Then we came back into the library. I folded up the copy of Bryce Diehl's will and filed it in my jacket along with the musket. That seemed to take a load off his mind. In exchange I left him the copy of Nancy's letter for his client's bedside reading. And then I looked at my ex-employer again, a last look.

He was still out.

It was just as well.

Sweet dreams, Twink babe, I told him in my mind, have a nice day.

I was on my way, but George S. Curie III was gesturing at me with the pages of Nancy's letter.

"One thing," he said kind of shyly. "Just out of personal curiosity, Cage, but what took you so long to get here with it? It's been over a week—ten days. When you didn't show up with it that night, and when Free . . . when Freeling didn't find it on you the next day, we thought . . . Well, we didn't know what to think."

I didn't bat an eyelash, but *Jeezus!* They really did think I'd had it all that time? Hard to believe, harder than hard. Unless they hadn't figured that even the Lonesome Cages of this world can fuck up now and then, not to say get their heads bashed in, or that they've got to sleep too every once in a full moon like ordinary human stiffs.

Well, far be it for me to have spoiled their illusions.

"So you locked the doors and windows?" I said. "And unplugged all the phones and settled down to *sweat* it out of me?"

"That's right."

"How come?" I asked him.

"Well, you hadn't delivered."

"But why didn't you try beating it out of me?"

"You've forgotten," he said with that grim prim smile of his, "I've worked with you before."

Yeah, George, I forgot.

"But what took you so long?" he repeated. "You don't mean to tell me you did it because you *enjoyed* it?"

He was staring at me like I was crazy. I must've been staring at him the same way. Then I burst out laughing. It was my first good laugh in a few thousand years or so. Hell, I all but clapped him on the back.

"Sure George," I told him. "That's right. I did it because I *enjoyed* it."

And then it stopped being so funny. Not funny at all, and my own laugh sounded a thousand years old.

I left him in the library, still shaking his head over it. All of a sudden I was too tired to care, to explain or not to explain, too bone tired even to say I looked forward to the pleasure of working with him again on some future project. I went out the front door and found the Mustang and drove west slowly all the way to the sea, and I smelled the mist a while, hoping it would blow the must out of my mind, which it did but only a little, and when finally I went home, the house was empty.

Epilogue

And like they say, that's all she wrote.

Whadda ya mean that's all she wrote? Wait a minute! Like who killed Karen? Like what happened to Robin Fletcher? Where's the solution, where's the justice? What kind of detective are you anyway, Cage, we want our money back!

Etcetera etcetera.

I can hear you screaming, friends. Oh yeah, all the way to Keokuk and back I hear you in the night. Well, at least you can't say I didn't warn you.

I know, I know, it's a lousy deal. Sure, and people are starving in Africa, and so on and so forth. Because I'll tell you something else you ought to have doped out by now:

This little book of mine, *Hush Money*, I didn't write it for you, or you, or you, no and not even for all the gang down at Eddie's All-Night Esso Station. It's a book with only one reader, friends. I guess you understand by now who that is.

Which isn't to say he hasn't been straight with me, so far. That next morning when the doorbell woke me up around noon, it was Miss Sensible Shoes herself, lorgnette and all, with the contracts in her satchel. I signed them and made her witness for me and lo and behold, the day IDH went public, what should I get in the registered mail but the first installment: one thousand shares of the blue chips, all made out to Cage's Triple-A Retirement and Pension Plan. The stock's been doing fine and so's the city of Diehl, ahead of schedule, way ahead of schedule. It looks like the biggest California grab of the California decade, maybe the California century, and I even see where George S. Curie III's got himself onto the reorganized Board, smiling his Cheshire smile for the cameras, so he must be doing fine too.

Sure, everybody's doing fine, all us grabbers. Twink Beydon's finally on his way to the Rose Bowl and like I say, I've no complaints . . . so far.

Only lately it's gone quiet again out here in Santa Monica, very quiet. And like you already know, when the quiet comes old Cage gets that chilly feeling in his gut, and he starts worrying about his insurance, and his insurance on his insurance. He starts to think that, now that Twink Beydon's smelling Roses, maybe he'll be telling himself he doesn't need all that interference after all, hell, that he can carry the ball across by himself. And he'll look around the field at all the stiffs who're supposed to be clearing out for him on the power sweep, one in particular, a pulling guard name of Cage who's standing around with his thumb up his ass clipping coupons, and he'll say: "What're we payin' all this deadweight for? That one there—" pointing at me "—the one with his thumb up his ass. What's his name?"

Sooner or later, Twink. Maybe not this year or next, but it's bound to be. I can read your mind, ole buddy.

After all, who wants a silent partner?

So I've taken out a little insurance, and you could call this book a reminder of premiums due. Not that you need worry, once you think about it. The way I've scrambled it up, it would take anybody else a month of Sundays to put the facts together, if they had one to spare. And they'd have to give the map of California a twist in the key places for all the balls to fall into their holes, and even supposing they managed that, what would they use for proof?

Speaking of which, Twink, I've made a small addition to Cage-to-Cage-to-Cage you ought to know about, just to round things off. In fact, in case you've been looking for me lately, I just got home from a trip up Seattle way. It took some doing—I mean, it happened two decades ago and when a guy nobody ever heard of falls out a window, who cares?—but you forget, that's my old stomping grounds up there, and the law's the law and mighty accommodating too when they sniff the green.

I got it, Twink. I found it under A for Accident and that's where they put it back, but in Cage-to-Cage-to-Cage I'm filing it under the M's.

So like I say, now everybody's happy, at least you and George S. Curie and me. So let's keep it that way. And when they get around to sticking up a plaque to you down at Diehl, tell 'em to put in a tip of the hat, down in the fine print, to very sincerely yours, B. F. Cage.

And as for all the rest of you stiffs and numbers out there on Robin Fletcher's Funny Farm, don't think I can't hear you pissing and moaning, you've been had, you've been gulled, you've been screwed and tattooed.

Sure you have.

Well, I'll tell you what I'll do. I'll lay it all out for you, what I've got, and you can take your choice. The who-killed-Karen bit, I mean. Probably you're not in the habit of solving puzzles when they don't print the answers in the back, but it's the best I can do under the circumstances. And if it's not enough, well, like I said, there's always Philip Marlowe, who'll be happy to do business with you if you can find him.

So here she goes:

NUMBER ONE

So Robin Fletcher was lying up one side of her mouth and down the other. It was easy for Robin Fletcher. Oh she was there all right up in Room 708, and maybe she was zonked like she said, or wasn't, it doesn't make a hell of a lot of difference. Because Robin Fletcher, even zonked, had been cool enough to (maybe) let Garcia have it in the eyeball, and cool enough to send me down more than one garden path. O.K. So suppose Karen was up there with her, looking out the window, doing what I don't know, maybe making up poems, maybe talking, talking about Andy or Daddy Twink or her grandfather's will, maybe even thinking out loud about what it would be like to end it all. Who can say, maybe even *hanging* out the window just to get the feel of it.

So Robin Fletcher helped her the rest of the way.

She had the motive, God knows. With one little push she could rid herself of one of her less favorite competitors and glom onto the wherewithal to make all her dreams come true. One little push. She had the cool too, that brand of Robin Fletcher cool which would have let her pick up the notebooks, the letter, and walk (not run) to the elevator, down and out, just like any old coed on her way to English 99.

Which is where I came in.

So Number 1 is for the Robin Fletcher fans, and let me tell you, Robin Fletcher's fans, you could do a lot worse.

NUMBER TWO

Number 2 starts out the same as Number 1: with Robin Fletcher lying again. I guess it just came naturally to the girl. Suppose Robin Fletcher *wasn't* there, but not ten miles away or fifty or a hundred or whatever it said in the friendly sheriff's file. More like, say, a hundred feet give or take a few, and straight down. Suppose she even *saw* Karen take her dive, what would she have done next? Well you or me, maybe we'd've started hollering bloody murder, calling down the law and so forth, but Robin Fletcher? No sir. Robin Fletcher would have walked right in to the elevator and up, and probably she would have passed him on the way, Garcia say, or Gomez, or anyone who belonged enough in Karen's life not to be noticed. (Not to be noticed? Hell, Jesus Christ Himself could have come and gone there, unnoticed, unless He started passing out the free samples.) And Robin Fletcher kept right on going, picked up her wherewithal before the law showed and then took off again to build up her alibi.

Who knows? Maybe she even got him to hold the elevator for her.

So Number 2 points the crooked finger at Big Daddy Twink Beydon, none other, he with the longest reach of all, with enough motive for a thousand murders and the cash to pay for them all and hush them up, and one in particular, buried back in his dark and dirty past, which would make Karen's plunge one hell of a Bell Fruit Gum coincidence if you tried explaining it any other way.

The more I think of Number 2, the more I think I'll hedge my bets on the verdict if push ever comes to shove and Cage-to-Cage-to-Cage has to drop the pumpkin.

NUMBER THREE

Number 3? Well, if I've got to go for Number 2 for purely professional reasons, there's still a tender spot in my heart for Number 3. It first came to me that Wednesday when I was signing my name on the dotted line, and if it sounded pretty far out when I heard it, I don't know, maybe there's some poet in me after all.

Because Number 3 is for the poetry.

Look at it this way. So Karie Beydon hated Twink, right? Hated him with every fiber of her scrawny body and always had, it was built in, so much so you'd have to say it had come to her straight down the chimney from her mother.

Right?

Right.

O.K., so on her twentieth birthday, two years late (not that it mattered), she got the birthday card from dear departed Nancy, which only confirmed what she'd always known in her screwed-up head. It put the fuzz on the peach, so to speak, the poison on the needle. And she went to see George S. Curie III just like the letter told her to, and George S. Curie III showed her the will, and she told George S. Curie III right there and then that she was going to put it to Twink just like Nancy had.

And maybe she even asked George S. Curie III what exactly had happened to her old man, her real one.

I mean it stands to reason, doesn't it? That she'd've been a little bit curious?

And George S. Curie III told her. Oh not in so many words maybe, and she might have had to worm it out of him like I did, but he'd have told her. Just like he told me.

So Karie went away and thought about it. And the more she thought about it, the more it seemed like she couldn't put it to Twink just the way Nancy had. Because where would have been the poetry in that? No, she had to come up with something different, something of her own. Her own thing.

And she did.

There wasn't any murder.

Karie Beydon jumped.

Do you see? That way nobody had to lie. Robin Fletcher could say, "She went out and I was too zonked to stop her." Twink Beydon could say: "I want to find out what happened to my daughter," and not be talking out of the corner of his mouth, only the side.

And I could say: Maybe we'll never know the whole truth and nothing but.

Poetry.

I'll say this much. You pays your money and you takes your choice, but if Number 3's the one and Karen Beydon did jump, then I've got to put in a good word for her here somewhere. Because the way it worked out, she sure did set it up for yours truly.

The astonishing true story of the world's #1 private eye

AVON
34694
$1.95

JAY J ARMES INVESTIGATOR

JAY J. ARMES AS TOLD TO FREDERICK NOLAN

He is the ultimate self-made man, the man with no hands, the most flamboyant and successful detective around. This is his electrifying life story—from the childhood accident that changed his life to the headline-making cases he's cracked, working for the likes of Marlon Brando, Howard Hughes, Elizabeth Taylor, Yoko Ono, and Elvis Presley.

"He talks a beautiful line of top-drawer private-eyes tales, the best of the season."
Kirkus Reviews

"Armes is an extraordinary character. Far more ingenious than the fictitious James Bond. . . . Read the book."
John Barkham Reviews

"IT'S A HELLUVA GOOD READ."
The New York Times

With 16 pages of photographs

JJ 11-77

THE EXPLOSIVE NEW BLOCKBUSTER BY THE AUTHOR OF FLETCH AND CONFESS FLETCH

FLYNN

He's a tough-talking Boston cop, a family man whose daughter just got a ruby pin from a guy named Fletch, and whose son was just fleeced of a violin.

FLYNN

And there they are, talking about rubies and violins when a plane explodes overhead. Burning bodies fall out of the sky—118 of them!

FLYNN

Aboard the plane were a Federal judge, a British actor, a middleweight champ, an Arab potentate—and, wouldn't you know it, a case for the formidable Flynn.

FLYNN

"Flynn is one of the smartest, gentlest, most sarcastic cops you'll ever meet."

The New York Times

FLYNN

BY GREGORY MCDONALD
TWICE WINNER OF THE
EDGAR AWARD FOR MYSTERY

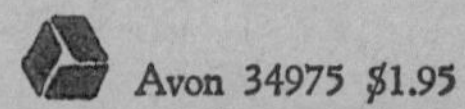

FLYNN 10-77